ON THE FRINGE:
A COLLECTION OF
COMMUNITY

*The Second Anthology by Write Club
of Mount Royal University*

Copyright © 2025
by Mount Royal University Write Club

All rights reserved. No part of this book may be reproduced in any form by any electronic or mechanical means including photocopying, recording, or information storage and retrieval without permission in writing from the author(s).

ISBN: 9798319240255
Independently Published
First Printing, 2025

Cover Design: Mazi Jade
Instagram: https://www.instagram.com/mazijadeart/

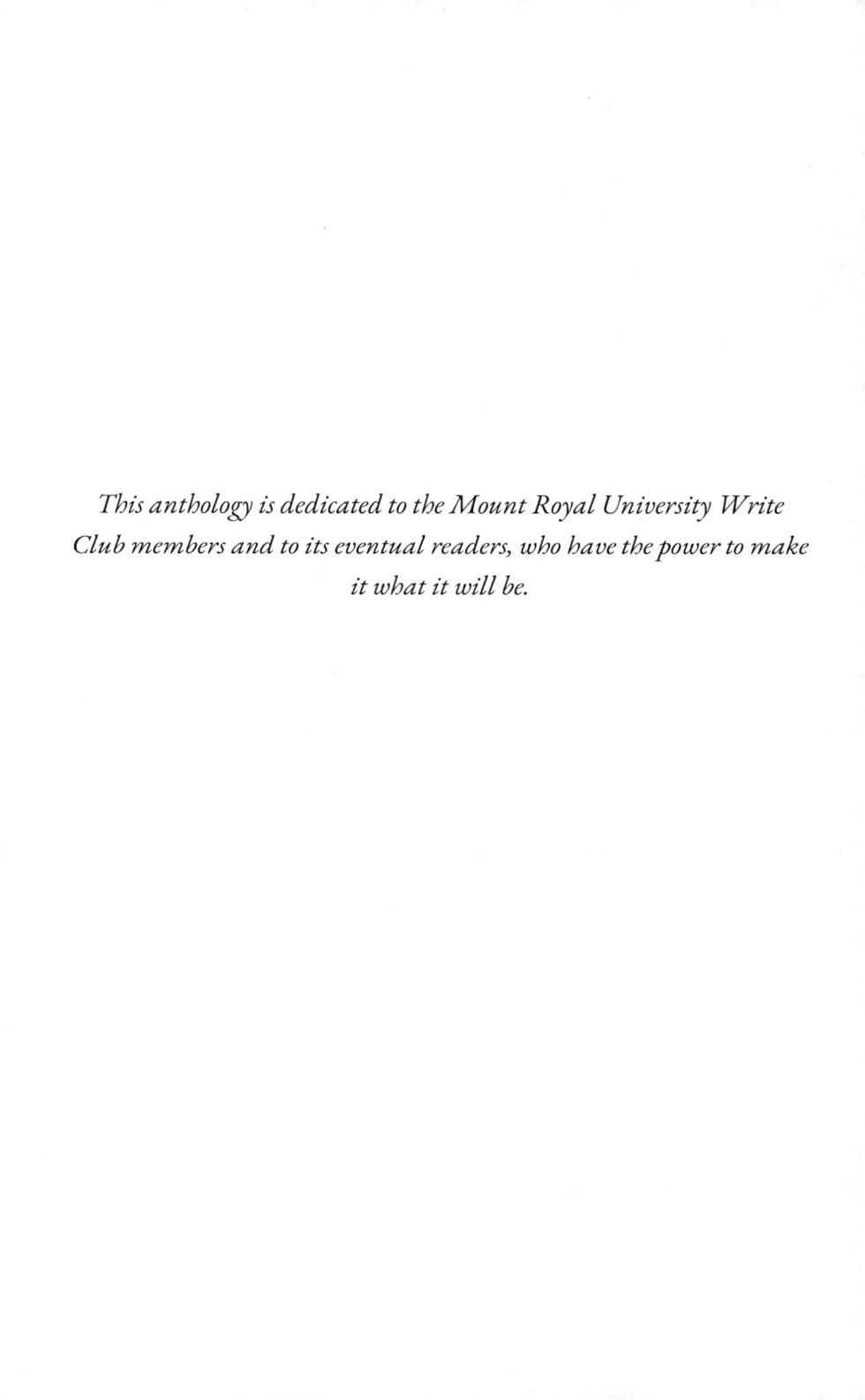

This anthology is dedicated to the Mount Royal University Write Club members and to its eventual readers, who have the power to make it what it will be.

TABLE OF CONTENTS

FOREWORD — 2

INTRODUCTION — 6

ARTIST PROJECT STATEMENT — 12

Part One: **TRADITION VERSUS CHANGE** — 13

    A Humble Colonialism by Ademola Adesola — 14

    It's Not Your Ears; It's the Dogma by Ademola Adesola — 16

    UNWROUGHT LIKE OXIDIZING COPPER by J.R. Adamson — 18

    Heart On My Sleeve by Ben Urquhart — 23

    Every Rendition of God Hates Us by Felix Da Costa Gomez — 35

    but i don't by Rachel Fitzgibbon — 40

    Death of a Snake Plant by Elle Nyitrai — 45

    The God Complex by Chandler Christie — 46

    A Cold, Undercooked Goose by Corbyn Andre — 56

    A Name is a Gift by Myra Monday — 68

    Heart of Stone by Teresa Anderson — 71

    The Witches Who Burned by Bailey J. Wilson — 80

    BLOODWRITING by Brennan Kenneth Brown — 85

Part Two: **COMPANIONSHIP** — 96

    The Ballad of Eve by Spencer Heindle — 97

forever, unconditionally by Spencer Heindle — 99

Anecdotes from a Hedonist by Felix Da Costa Gomez — 101

look back by Rachel Fitzgibbon — 111

The Gemini (An Homage to Old Gemini by Radical Face) by Bailey J. Wilson — 113

Ellie by Sylvia Belcher — 121

Darlene by Sylvia Belcher — 132

A Year Apart by Myra Monday — 137

Tracking in Eight Parts by Brennan Kenneth Brown — 140

"Dear Nina" by Mark (Marcus) Vertodazo — 148

"Dear Shan" by Mark (Marcus) Vertodazo — 150

"Limerence — A Triptych Series" by Mark (Marcus) Vertodazo — 152

Fog of the Lost by Levi Hunstad-Neighbour — 156

in sickness by Elle Nyitrai — 167

Strangling Blood Ties by Chau Luong — 169

Car Rides by Christina Jarmics — 177

The Expedition of Asbjørn Gunderson by Levi Lewko — 180

renaissance man by Elle Nyitrai — 197

Only Monster by Teresa Anderson — 199

If I am the moon, then you are the sun by Emma Marion — 202

I want to capture smells by Mel Perez — 204

Save Me a Seat by Rachel Fitzgibbon — 207

Daydreams by Dovonna Meloche	211
Part Three: **VISIONS**	212
A Spiraled Journey by Franz Valencia	213
The Script by Myra Monday	218
Purple Loosestrife Invasion by Brennan Kenneth Brown	220
I Love You by Christina Jarmics	223
Small Joys by Chau Luong	227
Building in Dead Sands by Morgan McLean-Alexander	232
Crimson by Sylvia Belcher	240
CONTRIBUTOR BIOGRAPHIES	253
ABOUT WRITE CLUB	261

FOREWORD

I've never been good at finishing what I start. Just a halfbreed high school dropout with every project abandoned, every relationship collapsing beneath my inconsistency—all of it trained me to expect failure. When I started Write Club in 2022, I had no leadership experience, but a hunger to create something that might outlast my own temporary presence.

A community.

We met in a too-warm library room, strangers passing prompts like prayers, sharing words still wet with birth. Ten names on a form. That was all.

Now, three years later, I stand at the edge of graduation, watching a community of over one hundred writers continue without me. We've doubled our executive team not because we need to, but because so many want to help tend what we've grown together. This book you're holding marks my last act as founder, my final foreword. The thought splits me open in the best way.

I keep returning to this image of forty people crammed into a room built for twenty, laptops open and so endlessly eager to write and share. A business major reading a poem about her grandfather's hands. An anthropology student becoming adept with the Haiku form. A nursing major finding language for what she witnesses daily.

Many didn't call themselves writers when they first walked through our door. Now they do. Now they are.

What happens in that room isn't magic—it's more fragile, more human. It's the slow, deliberate work of creating space where vulnerability becomes strength. Where a hesitant voice grows steady through practice, through witness. Where someone writes "I'm afraid" or "I remember" or "I want" and finds twenty people nodding, saying "yes, we see you, continue."

Writing saves lives. I know because it saved mine. During the pandemic when isolation pressed against my chest like a stone, writing gave shape to grief too heavy for me to carry alone. I started Write Club because I needed a place where words mattered, where the act of creating together might build something sturdy enough to stand against the storm.

We are at a crumbling edge. The climate crisis, political division, technological upheaval—we all feel the ground shifting beneath our feet. What do we do with our one wild and precious life when every system around us seems designed for collapse? We find each other. We make art. We bear witness. We remember that humans have always told stories to make sense of chaos, to find meaning when meaning seems impossible.

This anthology, centered on tradition, companionship, and visions, captures something essential about what we've built together. How we stand at the threshold between preservation and reinvention. Between the rituals that ground us and the changes that propel us forward. Between individual voice and collective witness.

I expected Write Club to fail like everything else I've touched. Instead, I've been taught leadership isn't about perfect stewardship but about creating conditions where others flourish without you. Plant seeds you won't be around to see bloom, build tables where everyone's voice carries equal weight.

When that business student—who once apologized before sharing her work—stood up at our last open mic and commanded the room with her words, I understood something fundamental: communities worth building are the ones that outlast their founders. Write Club was never meant to be mine. It belongs to everyone who has ever shared a prompt, offered feedback, organized a slam, or simply shown up with an open heart.

My Honours thesis focused on the power of students to transform educational spaces, but Write Club taught me what no research could—that when we make ourselves vulnerable to each other, when we risk failure and judgment to speak truth, we create refuge in a world increasingly built to separate us.

This is urgent work. The world is burning, yes—but it's also breaking open with possibility. When a first-year student whispers "I never thought I could write like this" or when a group of strangers becomes a family bound by words, I see how art creates sanctuary when nothing else can.

As many members know, I joke around a lot. But as I write this foreword, I sit at my desk, tears falling onto my keyboard, and I don't try to stop them. They are real. They are earned. They are mine. I am crying writing this because Write Club is the one good thing I've done that I haven't ruined. Because I'm graduating into uncertainty while watching something I love becoming more certain without me. Because beginnings always contain endings, and endings always hold new beginnings.

The best time to start writing was ten years ago. The second-best time is right now. These pages hold both invitation and promise—evidence that you, too, belong here in this gathering at the fringe, in the margins where the most interesting conversations happen, where community forms around our most honest words.

I am but one voice among many, and my hands tremble with gratitude. Thank you for showing me that what we build with love outlasts our own temporary presence. That our carbon dioxide, our breath, our being—it all becomes hope when shared. Thank you, thank you, thank you. I love you, I love you, I love you.

— *ken, founder.*

INTRODUCTION

About three weeks ago, in the Milky Way room, a usually over-crowded room full of free textbooks and coffee and greasy campus food, designed for and occupied by mostly over-tired and anxious humanities students who are supposed to be manically studying for their handwritten midterms and final exams on 18th-century literature, except that one business major who is always lingering, but I'm sorry to say, Faculty of Arts professors, is instead a completely collaborative space where juicy and bitter tea and gossip about romantic partners are shared, poetic howls about current political figures are exchanged, wispy snores are echoed by insomniacs, and passionate yet trivial discourses about the practicality of thinkers like Foucault are screamed, when Kenneth Brown, the president of the Mount Royal University Write Club, and my best friend and co-collaborator, Felix Da Costa Gomez, suggested I write the very introduction you are currently reading or listening to. I'll be honest, I thought they were joking. I think I remember I chuckled and said something along the lines of "there's probably someone more qualified than me." But then the realization set in that neither of them were joking with me. "No, you should totally do it." Their stern yet compelling eyes stunned me, stopping me dead in my self-conscious tracks. I shrugged my shoulders with a newfound confident grin on my face and said, "sounds great, I'll get right to it."

INTRODUCTION

When I went to my first Write Club meeting at the tail end of January 2023, I was a shell of who I am today, and I'm not being hyperbolic. I had just moved to Calgary from Langley, British Columbia, in October, transferred from the University of the Fraser Valley to Mount Royal University, and besides the two friends I had made in my creative nonfiction travel writing course who both somehow managed to convince insecure me to join Write Club, and I knew absolutely no one, yet, I was terrified to share myself with others and make more friends. I was petrified no one would care to know who I was and if I opened myself up, I would alienate myself further. Those two friends, Dorian and Danaë, had been asking me every week after class whether or not I was going to come, and every time they asked me I managed to find an excuse, mostly because I was terrified of feeling alone in a crowded room of forty people. I didn't want to be a talentless and tasteless intruder in an already established collective of incredibly talented writers and artists. I was not only insecure about myself, you know, because university does that to you and your self-esteem, but especially insecure about my writing. But that was until I ran out of believable excuses, and I had no choice but to go with them.

I remember my first meeting as if it were yesterday. I was sitting cross-legged on the carpeted floor in the back corner with Dorian. Dorian kept asking how I was and if I needed anything. I remained quiet and just smiled. The air was stuffy, lobs of snow were falling outside, and I was boiling on account of how many fiery and passionate individuals clacking away at their computer keyboards there were. Or maybe I just needed to take my thick sweater off.

INTRODUCTION

Kenneth started the meeting on the third floor of Wyckham house and he made us go around the room introducing ourselves and our writing interests. When he eventually came to me, I clammed up. I tried to say simply that I was interested in writing experimental fiction, but all I could say was I really liked William S. Burroughs, and I tried to write almost anything and everything, but I fumbled my words, tripped over them. I felt like an idiot. It didn't come out the way I had hoped, so I shut my mouth, darted my eyes into my lap, feeling completely embarrassed at myself and for the group. But then I looked across the room and saw a row of non-judgemental smiling faces. That was when I knew I had found myself in a special space, a space and group of interconnected people I wasn't used to or at least hadn't encountered before.

Kenneth gave us our first writing prompt, set a fifteen-minute timer and off we went. I don't remember what the prompt was exactly, but I remember instantly knowing what I was going to write about, and for the first time since being in university, feeling confident about my writing and my voice. The timer went off and Kenneth asked if there was anyone who wanted to share. Dorian violently nudged my shoulder and whispered, "You should share, dude." I shrugged my shoulders back at him, and hesitantly raised my hand, hoping Kenneth would just skip over me, but nope, he asked me to repeat my name again and share what I had written first. I took a huge gulp, and for the first time ever, read my creative work out loud to a group of people whose shared passion is writing other than my family, who, although being creative musicians, didn't give me what I needed when I shared my written work with them. I seem to remember the poem I wrote was about an anthropologist gone grave robber, but that isn't what is important; what is important is the response I received from the club, a response I now know isn't unusual in Write Club but was completely unexpected for me. People clapped, grinned, and gave me constructive yet wholly positive comments and criticism about my work. One person would make a comment and then another would build off the previous comment, so on and so forth.

Since high school, I hadn't been a part of a community-oriented artistic club, and even still, this just felt different, no other way of putting it. I could feel the joyous collaboration and sense of community pulsing in my tight chest and stomach. It was an embodied and felt sense of community, something I had yet to feel while pursuing my English Degree.

That was when I realized I had found a truly special and safe space and my community: a group of people and eventual collective of friends who not only gave me the confidence to share my work, but to be myself and share who I was with the ever-changing world around me. I know it sounds corny, slightly sappy, but I don't give two shits. That's what happened. They instilled a felt sense of confidence in me that I had lost when I moved to Calgary. A confidence that stayed behind in British Columbia and decided to taunt me everyday while I fought to find it again amidst the rubble.

That same night I heard my current best friend, Felix Da Costa Gomez, read out loud his poem, "Cave Dweller," which ended up being included in our debut collaborative poetry collection, *I'm*

INTRODUCTION

Just Waiting for Something to Happen, a collection of messy poems about coming into ourselves and finding a sense of community during a tumultuous time of social isolation, a collection wholly born, conceived, and edited within the confinements of the Write Club space, whether it was in the third floor of Wyckham or the Milky Way room, it didn't matter. The rooms might've changed, but the affective environment didn't.

The next day I stepped outside my comfort zone and messaged him on Instagram asking whether or not he wanted to collaborate together, and to my surprise he said yes, and from that not only did we manage to self-publish our first book together a year later, but a life-long friendship was founded, and for that I am eternally grateful not only to Felix for taking a leap of faith, but the program and community that is the Write Club apparatus. Without Kenneth and the Write Club community, I wouldn't have met my best friend, and most importantly, I wouldn't have found the community and friends that saved me, and I'm being serious here. Without Write Club, Kenneth, and the encouraging individuals and friends who come every Wednesday evening to hear and critique my wacky stories about body mutilation or Polish cannibals who eat their fathers or my self-deprecating poems about struggling to grow up, I probably wouldn't have dug myself out of the self-conscious crater that I was buried in. I probably wouldn't even be here today. This introduction wouldn't exist. Even thinking about that tears me apart. I love you all.

And you're probably thinking: "What does any of this have to do with this anthology? You're just a narcissistic shithead. Stop talking

INTRODUCTION

about yourself and get to the writers." And my answer to you is: everything. And I'm not trying to be narcissistic, nor selfish, I'm being completely honest and serious. I'm proud of what this club and anthology has done for me and countless others. This entire collection of poems about decolonization and learning to practice self-care and fictional tales of an individual's visions of being stuck in the cycle of samsara and nonfiction essays about writing with your blood and finding your best friend after being dumped by your childhood friend is the literal embodiment of my experience joining the Mount Royal University Write Club, and what it is all about: fostering community, challenging the sometimes harmful traditions which stifle us, and envisioning futures in which meaningful change can occur, social, personal, political, and so on.

If there is something, anything, moralistic to be learned or garnered from this exciting anthology containing fantastic and transcendental art by my lovely friends and unique community, let it be this: no matter your social or emotional state, join a community of people who bring you up, not down, and never be afraid to be yourself, even if you don't know who you are quite yet, nor know you'll never know.

Take care of yourself and surround yourself with people that love you and who encourage you to love yourself, even when you struggle to.

—Jake Beka, incoming Vice President of Publication

ARTIST PROJECT STATEMENT

Aside from just generally catching the viewer's eye, the artwork for this book's cover aims to capture and reflect the alluringly complex nature of emergence. I was extremely excited to make something expressive, organic, and detailed for this project. Something imbued with an energy of passion and fierce self-expression that would act as the fabric of the work itself. In line with some of the themes touched on by the many talented writers in this book, I embarked on a journey of exploring the human experience by giving space to my subconscious mind. Throughout the work you will find, the deeper you look, fragments of life's skeletal build. They are represented through simple shapes, varied repeating marks, and randomized symbols that interact with each other spontaneously to create, abstract, and even trivialize meaning. These forms adhere to and deviate from rules, order and conventional understandings of aesthetic balance. Ultimately, the interactions between the miscellaneous forms grow to represent a flowing balance of chaos, ever-moving, ever-expanding, and forever inviting the chance to experience something new at each glance.

—Mazi Jade, Artist of the Cover

Part One:
TRADITION VERSUS CHANGE

A Humble Colonialism
by Ademola Adesola

This land of maple leaves was never ours;
we purloined it!

Ours is a humble colonialism;
we're modest about our conquest.

We're generous landgrabbers;
look at the multitudes from many seas lapping up our generosity.

Multitudes mask our thievery;
multiculturalism is our watchword.

The more the merrier;
say it loud: The more, the more, ... Haaa... the more, the merrier!

We are the real rainbow nation;
motley races exist on these stolen territories.

All of us are equal;
but some are more equal than others.

Pure and white is our colour;

A Humble Colonialism
by Ademola Adesola

we are the polite police race;
the superior ones who know how to keep others *civilized*.

We are modest;
unlike our neighbor who boasts about their conquest.

We acknowledge our thievery;
we have out there the lollipop of reconciliation.

Let's get over the dispossession and loss of the *Residential Schools*;
join in celebrating our more-than-a-century-and-a-half humble colonialism! I wonder how I might wager my life tonight?

It's Not Your Ears; It's the Dogma
by Ademola Adesola

There's nothing wrong with your ears.
It's just that they aren't used to foreign tongues.

Your ears have been trained to recognize only the melody of familiar accents.
Like their owners, these ears aren't at ease with the strains of racial differences.

Why is it that I can hear and understand you, but you can't even hear me?
Is there something you need to learn about why your tongue isn't Babel to me?

There's neither refuge nor grace in the dilapidated edifice of 'It's my ears.'
Your ears aren't *Methuselah*; it's just that my heavy pigmentation reminds you of the odious dogma about me you're weaned on.

Being different from your kind can't be an excuse for you not to hear me.
You can hear and understand me if you reckon with my humanity.

It's Not Your Ears; It's the Dogma
by Ademola Adesola

You must see me as a human disserving of dignity.
Not as some inferior version of yourself, an aberration, and a specimen of how not to be.

Our differences aren't boulders of impassable borders.
Our unalikenesses are the colors we must use to create a rainbow of partnerships.

Quit denying the soundness of your hearing.
Start making efforts to be comfortable with my difference.

UNWROUGHT LIKE OXIDIZING COPPER
by J.R. Adamson

Unwrought like oxidizing copper and burnt-out—
He thinks it might be time for a change.
Unkempt like a malicious vagrant and strung out
at midnight on 20 mg of triple-action melatonin
and homegrown chamomile tea for a third year:

It's time for a fucking change.

I stare into the ugly boy
wearing a fraying corduroy cap
who needs to put on some weight
or at the very least workout twice a week
in the misty mirror who
wants to wake up dead
or feeling something different
or someone else entirely
and force his crumbly mouth into the shape of a smile,
for what I think is the first time in a long while.
He grabs hold of my slit wrists
and yanks them away.
I calmly place my nail-bitten hands on his face
and gently rub the black mold out of the bags

UNWROUGHT LIKE OXIDIZING COPPER
by J.R. Adamson

under his feeble copper eyes.

His distressed weeps dissolve into swirling ebony lagoons.
Tacky dye from dollar store pens and stinging poisonous lead
trickle like blazing rain into the stained bathroom sink
that fails to flower and bloom into metaphors and conceits.
He is unaware of his oozing corrosive artistry
and blames his lack of success on just being unlucky.
He is uneasy with the decadent opportunities
he has laid out for himself.
I gaze at the ugly boy
who wants to smash the murky glass
into hundreds and thousands of tiny shards
to use to slice his feeble fingers open
and tell him he looks good:

Try not to feel bad today.

Two cups of dark roast black coffee
every morning and afternoon—
and one 12 oz Corona every Friday night.
Oxidizing cement, once again,
degrading into unwrought asphalt.
Bereft sobs surging into
sluggish sienna stews
swimming with intoxicating silkworms

UNWROUGHT LIKE OXIDIZING COPPER
by J.R. Adamson

that slurry into sludge and spins into
sauntering sardonic moths
that tear slits in
the fabric of artistic creation—
cyclical like a non-linear
circular narrative.

It's like a cliché or literary trope
that's only become taboo
because we're all fucking sick of living it,
every day of
every month of
every year.

Like the recurring cliché
of grieving the loss of a loved one
or just flat-out feeling depressed
for no reason other than
you're just exactly that—
at least he knows it's going
to come back again every year,
like deciduous trees losing their brittle leaves
every fall and winter, and so forth.

Or at the very most, he has taught himself to expect it to.

UNWROUGHT LIKE OXIDIZING COPPER
by J.R. Adamson

He's been trying to change,
but he can't help himself.
Like Father, like son.
He's both the abused whimpering dog
snagged on a chain link fence with a rope,
and the drunk senseless abuser.
He's his Father's son.
He adores the death-driven-obsessed
fascist like poor old Plath did.

Daddy.

Except both his Father and him
are the Polish villagers crushed
by the Panzers and Tigers.
And he was grinded by his *Tata,*
and now he mangles himself to this day
with booze and books on wisdom traditions
written by a lama that got cancelled
because of sexual assault allegations.
Lapsing back into his learned
self-destructive habits
because they're all he seems to know:

Or are they?

UNWROUGHT LIKE OXIDIZING COPPER
by J.R. Adamson

I slouch in front of my computer
covered in dandruff and white dog hair,
and endlessly click and clack out
these faceless signs and hollow signifiers
that all fail to convey how I actually feel.
I gaze at the blurry boy
reflected on the bright screen, cowering,
covering his bloody and acne-littered face,
afraid of revealing his alluring and fetching
Virtue and Merit, like Sir Philip—
yet, still eager to make a name for himself,
to make something worthwhile of
his cyclical and formless existence.
Staring blankly at the fingerprint-smudged screen,
vacant and callous like a small town motel,
I wonder how I might wager my life tonight?

Heart On My Sleeve
by Ben Urquhart

2008

When I was 6, my grandpa took me for a walk. A rarity: between my mom's parents, it was always Nana who took my brother and I on walks, always on the same path to the west. We'd go left down the hill and pass by three ponds, each bigger than the last, and eventually reach the lake. Nana would give us both a little container of rice crackers, and my brother and I would race around the playground. Grandpa took me right instead of left, a miniscule action that felt impossibly taboo. That feeling grew as he took a cigar out of his pocket and drew it to his lips, only to pause before he lit it.

"Don't smoke." Grandpa cautioned me sternly. He was from China, but his spoken English was perfect: his voice was a slow baritone with a slight accent. Every syllable had an unconscious weight to it.

"Only for something special." He added as an afterthought. Grandpa took out his lighter, an old-fashioned silver one that gave a satisfying clink when he flipped the cap back. He took a couple puffs: smoke curled out from his gray teeth, rose up his tanned face, beyond the mole on his right cheek, past his snow-white hair. He cut a striking figure: he was tall, especially for a Chinese man, with broad shoulders and a serious face. Not bulky, but soft in the stomach like old people were. Nana and Grandpa always dressed nice, even casually—

something my mom inherited. From afar, they looked regal. But whenever I talked to Grandpa, he'd break out into a roguish grin while he listened to what I had to say. Then he'd pause and stare through me for a pregnant moment while he formulated his thoughts. He always emphasized the first word of a sentence with a little more punch, a little more oomph.

From afar, a stone-faced monolith. Up close, he was just Grandpa.

I wondered if I would ever be like him.

A weak breeze blew, and I got a whiff of the smoke. I wrinkled my nose and made a disgusted expression in the way only small children can.

"That smells weird," I said earnestly. "Does it taste good?"

Grandpa laughed, like I'd told an excellent joke.

2017

My Dad owned an old JDM Forester, a dark-green car he affectionately deemed "the Gumpster". It was a stick-shift, something I didn't pick up on for a long time. I was the ignorant kind of passenger: I preferred to read my book, or stare blankly into the void while I daydreamed of comics and video games.

"It has a stick shift on the left?" I asked him one day while he was cooking dinner. He nodded. "Isn't that hard?"

Dad chuckled, a deep rumble that permeated through our house. His voice could fill up a room: perfect for conference calls. Maybe a little too perfect; I'd been woken up more than once by him talking on the phone or computer. When he laughed in the movie theatre, I could always hear him over everyone—something that embarrassed me slightly.

His voice matched his six-foot-three frame, still lean in his 50s from a lifetime of exercise. Dad knew anything about everything, a bastion of order amidst chaos. A larger-than-life presence.

I guess after Mom died, he had to be.

The stick shift on the left would be hard, Dad explained, except he already had practice doing it. Back when he was a kid, Grandpa would steer with one hand and pack his pipe with the other. Dad would shift gears from the passenger seat so Grandpa could smoke while he drove.

I laughed. "That seems a little dangerous."

"No," Dad agreed, and his smile faded slightly. "Your Grandpa did a bit of not-smart stuff back in the day."

I didn't know how to respond—how to acknowledge that my grandparents were anything less than perfect people who doted on my brother and I—so I left it at that.

6 years later, I took edibles with my roommate and went to see the Barbie movie. We laughed way too loud at every joke, and I realized---to my horror and delight---I sounded exactly like my Dad.

NOW

I can't remember what my mom sounded like. I try to recall her voice, but it's been a decade since I talked to her. Sometimes I dream she's alive, and when I wake up I just lie there and try to fall asleep so I can see her for a little longer.

The only thing I can perfectly remember is her saying "goodbye Stinkerdoodle". That's how she ended the goodbye video she made, something she created five months before she died. Mom said it so lightly, like it wasn't the last thing she'd ever tell me.

I miss her.

2022

I smoked pot for the first time at 20. Daring, I know. My friends had pissed me off, really pissed me off. I deal with unresolved emotions by not dealing with them, so I decided to spend my Friday night smoking with my stoner friend. The act of smoking is terrible. It's an ashy thing, cinders and fumes, a little cylinder filled with a burning plant and boy does it taste like it. Acrid air filled up my chest, burning and clawing when I expelled it. Every stutter in my breathing was another invitation to cough. How Clint Eastwood makes this look cool was beyond me.

I tilted my head up to look at the falling snow: a shifting constellation of white, tiny stars plummeting out of their place in orbit, dying heat death on my skin. The streetlamps glowed a dull yellow overhead, and the brick of the apartment building stretched stories above me. If the light pollution wasn't there, could we see the stars beyond the snow? That would be something: a constellation beyond a constellation.

"How am I supposed to feel?" I asked.

Heart On My Sleeve
by Ben Urquhart

"I don't know," She thought for a moment. "Like, fuzzy?"
I took a drag. "Fuzzy."

Smoke billowed out my mouth, shrouding her heart-shaped face for a half-second, and all I wanted was this drug to make my brain and heart and face line up—perfect emotional awareness and expression—to give me all the answers: an epiphany condensed into a little brown pre-roll. But no epiphany was coming, just fuzziness, white noise in my cranium.

This wasn't special at all.

We finished the joint and went up to her apartment, where I proceeded to hack up a lung. I stood in her tiny kitchen for 15 minutes, drinking an obscene amount of water. Every itch in my throat was another sip. When the scratching in my larynx finally subsided, I noticed her Halloween candy. I ate every single Swedish Fish she had.

"I don't feel high." I told her seriously. She just giggled.

When I fell asleep that night, it was without answers and more than a little confusion. Two months would pass; I'd fight with my first roommate and realize how much I struggle with expressing myself. I thought I wore my heart on my sleeve, but somewhere between my brain and my face is a disconnect that means I express about 3% of my emotions. And talking about how I feel is even worse.

I look at photos of Mom and Dad---with her toothy grin and his close-lipped smile that looks more polite than joyful—and I think I know where I got it from. If you knew my dad, you could tell he's happy. If you didn't, you'd think he was just grimacing for the camera.

My expression, or lack of one, is probably hereditary, and I doubt the death of a parent at the age of 12 did anything to help my disposition. My monotone face and voice lead to some funny miscommunications, but it still hurts when my friend says I just talk at you until I elicit an emotional response.

    I'm right here, can't you see me?

2023

    My brother and I were screaming at each other. I made a wrong turn in the work truck because he refused to give directions. I was half-focused on navigating out of the suburb, half-focused on creating the cruelest insult possible. The AC was on full blast yet my skin was boiling, like my rage would melt me from the inside until I said my piece. My brother sat sullenly in the backseat—Google Maps pulled up on his phone—but he wouldn't read it to me.

    My coworker was sitting beside me, a nervous grin on his face: "I think the heat's getting to us," he said with trepidation. It was a clear out if my brother or I wanted it. But I craved conflict, constantly fantasizing about an outlet for my ever-present anger. My ego couldn't let him have the last word.

    "No," I replied to my co-worker, but I was glaring at my brother through the mirror. "I think he just needs to quit bitching and own up to something for once in his life."

    My brother screamed back, and sick satisfaction flooded through me because I could keep taking my fury out on him. Afterward, like every time I get mad, all I felt was shame and self-loathing roiling around in my gut. I forced out an apology because I hate conflict, even if I fantasize about it. He still gave his two-week notice that afternoon.

Once we stopped working together, our relationship returned to normal: occasional movie nights and the odd conversation when I popped into my dad's house. There's still a lot I don't know about him. My other coworker told me my brother said he had "the occasional drunk cigarette at the bar". I didn't even know he smoked. Or that he went to bars.

I envy my brother in some respects: he doesn't care about outside opinions and he's not afraid to question authority. I'm a bit of a pushover and a people pleaser. I have a hard time saying no or accepting a compliment without self-deprecation. I do nice things for my friends because it's easier than saying I value them. Nice things make people happy, and if everybody's happy then I should be happy too.

I tried that approach after Mom died: making sure everybody was happy, not myself. It didn't work so great. I didn't realize I fell back into that habit.

I asked my brother if he was okay with me writing about him. He said yes, as long as it was a "flattering depiction". We share the same brand of sarcasm.

I'll say it here, for all the times I never said it to your face: I love you.

2024

    I was 22 when I bought cigarettes for the first time. I hope by now it's clear I wasn't a very adventurous youth. It felt wrong, like the first time I went to the casino or applied for a passport. An experience reserved for adults, something I rarely consider myself. I think that when I turned 18, my definition of adult just moved up to people over 30. I know they don't have everything figured out: they're just better at hiding it than me.

    I bought them at 7-Eleven, the one just off Parkdale Boulevard with the dilapidated parking lot and the hellish curb that smacks my front bumper when I pull out wrong. I walked up to the cashier and tried to project as much rugged charm as I could, knowing damn well I have a baby-face.

    "I'd like some cigarettes please." I asked.

    The cashier looked back at me, bored. "Which ones?"

    I decided honesty was the best choice.

    "I dunno," I admitted. "I've never bought them before. Which ones are cheapest?"

    She looked back at me blankly and grabbed a carton to show me: it was decorated with a photograph of a man's cancered throat and voice box.

    "Perfect." I replied.

    Sixteen bucks later (seriously, sixteen?) I was smoking with two buddies on my apartment deck. None of us had smoked before—I wanted to try it. It was marginally better than smoking weed. But my head was rushing, there was a familiar burn in my throat, and I was queasy enough that I needed to sit down. The three of us gathered around the kitchen counter and discussed our experience like a post match analysis of a sports game. They liked it, I didn't. I went to throw the pack out, but they told me to keep it, "just in case".

I don't feel like an adult when I smoke. I feel like a teenager about to be caught doing something bad. Sometimes I joke that I still feel like I'm 14. I'm only half-kidding. Some days I feel like a child running around in the dark, waiting for someone to turn on a light and guide me to my destination. I'm in a body that's too big for me and I want a parent to tell me what to do so I don't have to think for myself. There's a shameful comfort in following instructions.

Two weeks later, my second roommate broke up with his girlfriend. He trudged downstairs and quietly announced he was going to smoke on the deck, his way of asking not to be alone. I lit up a couple darts in solidarity and we stood side-by-side with our arms on the balcony, staring off into the night. I looked at the inky black expanse and examined the burning cylinder in my hand, doing anything but watching my roommate while he talked. That made things easier somehow.

Men are allowed to express themselves now but being allowed to and knowing how to are very different things, so we talked matter-of-factly without displaying any of the emotions we're discussing. He can't sleep, his appetites gone, and I'm reminded that despite his rough exterior, my roommate really feels. Last night he wanted something from the kitchen but never came downstairs because he didn't want me to see him "like that". I offered a hug and told him I don't care if I see him crying. He was still uncomfortable with that, so I offered to wait in my room if he needed the kitchen while he's emotional.

It's easier to work around these things than to change.

Somewhere along the way something broke in my head and I struggle to offer myself the kindness I give others. Self-loathing, self-disgust, emotional constipation, masculinity: I can't pin down the root cause. When I see a friend crying, I want to help. When I cry, I think I look pathetic.

My brain tells me to man up and just keep moving until it gets better. And it always does, but the dogged march forward never gets any more pleasant.

My running theory is societal standards from my dad's generation and his dad's generation. If a boy cried, he would probably get beat or called weak, because his parents weren't 'raising a girl'. That's changed somewhat, and it's far more socially acceptable to express emotional issues as a man, but the residual preservation instinct remains. I'm confused because I was subject to a loving childhood, yet I'm still emotionally closed off.

At the beginning of 2024, whenever my friends asked me how I was doing, I would just say good. I didn't want to explain that it was about to be the tenth anniversary of my mother's death, I was quitting Prozac and the withdrawals wouldn't let me think straight, I had a weird lump in my left pec and I was scared it was cancer because my Mom had cancer, my roommates were fighting, my elbow had been aching for months, I couldn't get over a girl, I was depressed, skipping classes, and having a quarter-life crisis over the fact that I would graduate in a year.

In my worst moments, I didn't understand why people cared about me.

Then one day I was sitting with two people in A&W after a meeting with our school newspaper, and when my friend asked me how I was doing, I told the truth for once. And he accepted me.

Another night, I broke down in front of a roommate. Ugly, heaving sobs about my mom and how it had been a decade since I saw or heard her. He'd broken down in front of me once: I had offered him a hug. He declined, citing his dislike of physical contact and settled for a pat on the shoulder.

When I was done crying, despite his hatred of them, he gave me a hug.

The dogged march forward is better with company.

NOW

I laid awake one night and tried to pin down what I thought constituted manliness. Then I tried to think of what constituted womanliness. I ticked off the exact same boxes and realized maybe I'm just trying to identify what makes a good person.

I'm bound by incoherent and intangible rules of gender, but like my dad wisely pointed out to me, I choose what I hold onto and let go of.

Sometimes I feel like I've skated through life on the kindness of others. But what is kindness if not giving yourself away for nothing in return? Ultimately, the validity of that statement changes nothing. Either way, I'm still here: beautiful and imperfect, like my dad and grandpa.

There are a hundred core memories I'll never forget and a million more I'll never remember. Maybe those core memories were the crystallization of every choice leading up to a crucial moment: maybe I just remember them because of some arbitrary detail.

Some days I dream of people I miss and they tell me everything I want to hear, and I regret waking up because fantasy is better than reality.

Other days I shout along to the music in my car and my monotone expression shatters into an idiotic grin because I'm alive.

Every Rendition of God Hates Us
by Felix Da Costa Gomez

Blockbuster walks from the park
before the crimson Netflix logo
and its signature "dun dun" as a
precursor to unwatched, overpriced
movies and my tongue in your mouth with
awkward shoulder glances in case your dad
comes jogging down the stairs

Enthralled by the yellow bold letters and
the blue billboard sign, I was too late to
jump down from the van and the automatic
door slid closed on my leg

I started crying as I sat on the rim of
my mother's van because I thought the
door was going to gnaw through my leg and
leave me nothing but a gushing red stump and
my mother rubbed my hair and told me it was
okay even though I was being stupid

The aisles with neatly packed movie
Dvd's and the rental consoles stowed away

Every Rendition of God Hates Us
by Felix Da Costa Gomez

behind massive glass doors, I remember
walking here with my brother and forcing him
to rent Shrek 2 the video game and he beat the
game in one sitting just for me, even though he
wanted to rent out Arkham Asylum

The backyard where my sister taught the
neighborhood immigrant girls how to speak
English because she knows what racism feels like,
the Esso station residing on the first curb to the
left, a three minute walk from our house

Sugar covered teeth and greasy cheap pizza
slices with the stringy cheese previously frozen
sticking like a pest to your irritated red gums

It was an Esso before a 7 Eleven because the big
man up top likes capitalizing in the southern suburbs
because he thinks rebranding gives Evergreen an identity

Hanging with my sister's friends in the summer
because I had friends at school, but none
of them liked me enough to make jokes outside
of third grade math class

Traversing through wooden fences, a pilgrimage

Every Rendition of God Hates Us
by Felix Da Costa Gomez

from Evergreen to Millrise past that Chinese owned
Movie rental gas station where my parents got me
Star Wars 1-6 for my tenth birthday

It sits right next to Tom's House of Pizza next to
a spacious soccer field hidden under mounds of
tall grass, but they probably ruined it by now by
filling space they deemed empty with a school
because to those people, the men that live outside
of the suburbs, that's all an open soccer field is; empty space

Money speaks louder than memories.

The compact, hissing hot computer systems
sitting under the shitty black monitors in the
computer lab where we played Poptropica and
Animal Jam and Roblox are now great ancestors to
my Ryzen 9 5900x 32 gigabyte ram system
that can refresh a page in less than a second

The gym at St. Bonaventure Junior High School
holds the remnants of my DNA in the torn skin
of my knuckles- Belly Baseball and watching the
chubby kid nearly get his head crushed because he
stood under the mat during clean up duty

Every Rendition of God Hates Us
by Felix Da Costa Gomez

Conversations at the tiny green lockers outside
of our Grade 8 homeroom about who was hopping
online later and you asking me "Hey man, can your
mom give me a ride?" and me wanting to respond with
"No, this is the fourth time this week, I want to get home
early for once and my mom is tired of your shit, go fuck
yourself you leach bitch" but saying yes instead because
I didn't want to see the expression on your face if I said no

Writing and drawing lewd Pokemon parodies in the arts
classroom and selling them for ten cents a pop before
finding out that "Chodemander" didn't exactly appeal
to twelve year olds or the school principal but he just
had a bad sense of humor

Giving my mom two months worth of allowance
money and asking her to buy the newest Diary of
a Wimpy Kid volume and finding it on my bed
after coming home from school

Giving my mom five months worth of allowance
money and asking her to buy Omega Ruby and finding
it on my bed after coming home from school

Poptropica, Hotel Habbo, and Webkinz before
hundreds of hours spent on Steam achievements

Every Rendition of God Hates Us
by Felix Da Costa Gomez

Watching Shonen anime by misogynist incels where
the women all have double d-cups before rotting to porn
Greg Heffley as the biggest loser on earth before
writers decided to turn losers into underdog heroes

Take me to a Scholastic book fair
Take me to a Blockbuster
Take me to Build a Bear

Explain to me how people are not God in
their nature to create things and do away
with other things, try to convince me that
every rendition of God does not hate us

Students are God
Teachers are God
People are God
Corporate is God

So the next time I walk to that
boarded up building with the forgotten
blue sign and yellow letters, do not try
to convince me that every rendition of God
does not hate us

but i don't
by Rachel Fitzgibbon

Time is a fickle thing

It stretches out, long and languid
Only to fold back over itself
Days which last forever turn into months that pass too soon
Years blur by with nothing to distinguish them from one another
Except that it is never the same as the year before
Different snow falls, different leaves sprout
But the pattern remains the same
I remain the same as

January ices over into February, slow and shivering
My blood freezes, coagulates inside my body
Red tipped ears and runny noses are the only proof of life
The worst is over and yet it is just getting started
The icy wind hits hard, the weak winter sun cannot soothe the hurt as

February tips into March, and I am not ready
Days gain length, steady and slow
A last deep breath of frigid air before the world melts
Soon the days will stretch out like taffy,

but i don't
by Rachel Fitzgibbon

the thick summer sun will burn
But the snow still under my feet refuses to be forgotten as

Winter jerks into spring, In stops and starts
A false warmth in the wind turns back to frost
It never gets easier to have comfort ripped from your hands
Winter is relentless, even knowing that spring always comes
Holding the world tight in its icy grip, even as

March melts into April, rushed and frantic
Too much happens, too quickly
More hours in the day, more sun in the sky,
More heat on my face, and still not enough time
Winter is slow and lethargic but spring moves too fast as

April grows into May, insistent and solid
Pushing up through the thawed ground
And Everything comes back to life except for me
I remain frozen, in stasis, catatonic
The wheels of time move ever forward as

May leaves me in the dust, catapulting into June
And I can do nothing but watch it leave
Flowers bloom while I sit and rot
My scent of decay permeating the place
Sped along by the ever growing heat as

but i don't
by Rachel Fitzgibbon

Spring dissolves into summer, hot and sticky sweet
Like the fairground cotton candy from youth
Gone quickly and leaves you with an ache in your gut
The last sparkling pieces of ice long melted
Under the screaming sunshine as

June burns into July, like my shoulders on a summer day
Sensitive and painful, peeling like skin
Half a year gone and nothing has changed
Except for the very world itself
Who has died and been born again as

July spills into August, sticky sweet hands losing grip
Like the lemonade I dropped all over my lap
Scrubbed my skin raw to rid myself of the tack
And still residue resides on my thighs
Summer lingers as

August gives in to September, and I dig in deeper
I see winter on the horizon and try to push back
The relief from the heat is lost in the dread of the cold
I have only just thawed
And now I must prepare to freeze again as

Summer slips into fall, Sleepy and slow and then quickly crisp
The leaves shifts hues and detach from their branches

but i don't
by Rachel Fitzgibbon

The sun hangs lower in the sky
The darkness of the night eagerly chasing it away
The temperature steadily dropping as

September becomes October, steady and sure
There is nothing to be done
I cry and scream and rage
And winter advances nonetheless
Getting closer and closer as

October withers into November, bare and miserable
Naked trees shake in the howling wind
And goosebumps rise on my flesh
I wrap myself in misery like a heavy wool sweater
Attempting to melt my frozen soul as

Fall congeals into winter, wicked and cold
Leaves rot under snow as the day remains grey
And time loses meaning under the dark afternoon sky
A losing battle against death and decay
The unlovely season wins again as

December shoves past November, gaudy and loud
Faux lights which fight against the omnipresent dark
That suffocating and all encompassing blackness

but i don't
by Rachel Fitzgibbon

Which makes me forget that the sun ever shone on this wretched place
An artificial month, filled with everyone else's excitement as

December barrels into January, a fresh start to do it all again
A year gone with nothing to show except my claw marks from trying to stop time
Every new year the same as the last, nothing changes even as everything does
Sick and the same

Time is fickle that way

Death of a Snake Plant
by Elle Nyitrai

in the corner of my bedroom sits a plastic pot,
painted to appear terracotta, from it grows a snake plant
once belonging to my mother, her mother before
survival long surpasses a quarter-century expectancy

they promised it was no mortal being in my care
yet ever since the relocation, the foliage does not appear
to have been seduced by charmer's music, upright nor proud
jutting downward so desperately
it must desire to slither across my floor

the mirror image of medusa on days unkempt
coloured as if she was a heartbroken girl
running hands across her scalp
hydrogen peroxide at her fingertips

i ask my mother what i'm doing wrong,
maintaining the oath to love this houseplant dearly,
she tells me to coddle is to suffocate,
it's gotten used to thriving off neglect
yet i do not resist the impulse
i overwater it

The God Complex
by Chandler Christie

On Maypril 41st, 3025, I made the decision that I was going to kill the LORD. This wasn't just a light decision I came to suddenly; I've had it for quite some time now during my stay at the colony. To nearly any other worshipper of the LORD, this idea would have seemed like just an edgy remark from a malicious middle-schooler, but my intent grew stronger the longer I was subject to the hollow conditions of living aboard the migrating colony for so long. To be exact, my grievance wasn't specifically directed at the LORD himself, moreso the conditions that had developed stemming from his influence; if you weren't a follower, you were as obsolete as an unmarked grave.

Discontent aboard the colony was present, albeit hushed to barely a registering above a whisper. I was sure some of my coworkers questioned whether the LORD resided on Colony premises at all, though none of them would outright state it. My decision to kill the LORD was finalized after the most recent doctrine was proclaimed over the colony's intercom:

"This is a message to all faithful colonists: In order to keep the population at an even level, all adulterous material will be prohibited from colony premises from now on and all transmissions from earth will be screened for any breach of this doctrine."

That was when I decided I'd had it. As if life on this dreary crater wasn't empty enough without any recreation apart spending all day fulfilling work orders, which couldn't just be done by the computers for some reason; but now it seemed that high council was intent on keeping everyone from straying from "the path of the LORD." This wasn't even the first time one of the LORD's proclamations felt overtly egregious, I recalled hearing the intercom announce: "In order to reduce the amount of waste going through waste disposal, we are limiting the number of shipments one can receive from earth on a monthly basis" on the morning I was expecting a gift from my mom back from Earth, though I probably shouldn't have gotten my hopes up after the most recent doctrine from 3 days prior to that, which was: "Do not permit those residing outside of the scope of our fair colony the privilege of partaking in it's blessings, nor should you mistake the indulgences from outside the colony as anything less than distractions to mislead you from our great path."

When I first learned I would be permitted to live aboard the floating colony, I thought it was a joke. During my life on Earth, I was far from the most devout follower of the LORD, and, supposedly, the only way to guarantee yourself passage aboard the colony was to have some sort of close relationship to a high councillor. As an unmarried 28-year-old tech-support worker with only a game console, a handful of games, and a few raunchy books to my name, I didn't pretend like I had any significant chances of landing a position aboard the colony. But, as fate would have it, the stoogey owner of my apartment building (who also just so happened to be a high councillor) was planning on renovating the entire building to turn into executive suites and I, along with several other of his tenants, were moved to live aboard the colony. I might've considered it a miracle, had the conditions for our departure to spend our time organizing work request orders aboard the colony not been disclosed.

The promises to earth advertised by the Council of the Lord rung back through my mind: "Experience the gifts of the Lord's Universe on the first migrating space colony!" I'll admit, there was something more concrete to their promises of salvation compared to the other would-be startup sects of the time trying to garner up followers in the financial turmoil of life of the late 29th century; likely it had something to do with the extra stellar gospel of the LORD being heavily outspoken by industry veterans who had somehow remained stable at that time. Given the massive economic collapse that had supposedly made life on earth a waking nightmare, so it made some sense that the population back then were willing to fall under a voice from the sky, not even questioning why the plan for salvaging earth involved developing floating colonies out in space.

Even my own mother, who had maintained the business-sense to brush off every would-be prophet desperately pleading outside her door to offer her soul for salvation, had given in to the assurance that salvation was possible beyond the scope of the earth. She was ecstatic when I told her I'd been allowed to move to the colony. "Oh! Bless Stewart that Landlord of yours! You're going to be safe with the LORD! This is the happiest I've been in years!" These were the last words I'd ever heard from her before I left, "Do your best while you're up there! I won't be there, but the LORD will!" Before I left, she gave me a parting gift: it was an old calendar back from when I'd graduated high school. Back then there were still only twelve months, before the Order of the LORD adjusted the yearly cycle to have seventeen. To most people, this would have seemed useless, but to me this was special. Partly because every page had a spread of partially-clothed women posed in provocative positions, which frustrated my mom at the time, especially when I'd forgotten to bring it with me when I'd moved out. Knowing that, her giving it to me with my moveout date still circled on it made the gift even more meaningful.

    I had the calendar placed up in my quarters for the entirety of my tenancy, looking at it now only solidified my resolve. I had a scheme calculating in my mind almost immediately. I left my designated residence early and made my way to scrap management. Bill, an acquaintance I'd gotten familiar with over time, was stationed there for the day, although we generally got along well, it took some convincing to get him to lend me a discarded spark taser and repair it back to working quality. Only those with higher privilege were granted the opportunity to carry one, to maintain "safety" aboard the colony, though one would think such a highly valued object wouldn't be discarded so easily. I promised I wouldn't use it out in the open, and I would keep that promise, for the most part.

    Now, all I had to do was ensure I'd be granted an audience with the LORD. Supposedly, you could be granted an audience through proving your devotion, though that opportunity was sparsely granted and would be far too time-consuming. I had to utilize a more immediate method through committing a questionable crime of character. If I felt like it, I could have taken the time to plan something more elaborate, but that felt unnecessary, so I allowed my impulse control to falter for this.

I entered my sorting division center, a bit later than usual for added influence, and walked past the dismal workstation I had been expected to sit at for the remainder of the day. The supervisor, the ornery man named Stewart whose bulbous face was beet-colored by nature, started barking his typical drivel at me to get back to my station; I ignored him, instead marching directly right up to him and, in full view of the entire calculating force, wrapped my lips around his and started sucking. I'll admit, I'd had better intimate experiences in my life, though no one would argue I wasn't putting in any effort.

The time it took for me to be apprehended and hauled through the colony's workforce center to the central operating facility was quicker than anything else I've ever witnessed being processed in my time at the citadel. Stewart's fiery red face hadn't cooled down by the time he joined the rest of the high councillors in their judicial blue robes. I was brought into the center of the round amphitheatre, with the seventeen high councillors surrounding me at all sides around the perimeter of the room. A circular panel in the ceiling opened, and the console of the LORD descended down into the room through a pillar of white light. Its screen beamed over me and illuminated the entire room in a white glow, the sounds of computing and processing filled the air like a choir. Through the wide speakers on the two sides of the LORD's console. His voice echoed out like an opera.

"*For what reason have I been summoned?*"

The God Complex
by Chandler Christie

To make my move right now would've been too hasty, I had to wait for the moment where everyone in the room would be off-guard. I just stood quietly as the First Elder of the high council stepped forward and proclaimed: "Hail divine LORD, we bring you a heretic deserving of your judgment and sentencing."

"*And what are the crimes of which the heretic is accused of?*" The LORD asked,

"Heretic is accused of: assault, workplace misconduct, and disrespect of authority." The First Elder declared.

"Excuse me, I have a name!" I spoke up.

"You will be silent in the presence of the LORD and his court!" Another High Councillor demanded,

"Oh come on! Whatever happened to innocent until proven guilty?!" I argued, "Don't you want to know the cause of my *blasphemous* behaviour so you can curb it in others going forward?"

"You have no authority to make such demands of this council!" The First Elder argued.

"*Hold, Councillor. I allow for this heretic to speak for himself. His insight will be informative of my judgement.*" The LORD declared.

"But, milord, this is unconventional of council procedures!" The First Elder insisted, "He has relinquished his authority to speak by desecrating the lifestyle about our colony!"

"See! This is the problem here! You've all completely disregarded how life was on earth that you'll willingly reduce any semblance of earth customs here just to perpetuate some notion that life up here is so great because it's not earth!" I interjected.

"Mind your words, heretic! Our colony is a sanctum of divine strength that honours the great LORD who lifts humanity away from their purgatory on earth into the heavens of the stars! To speak against the LORD's mission is to speak offense to the universe itself!"

"*Hold, I have not yet made my judgement.*" The Lord of All insisted, "*Tell me this, from where does your fondness of Earth arise in such a way that encompasses the divine significance of the colony?*"

"Oh, I wouldn't say it quite like that," I responded, "In fact, I'd have about as many complaints living on earth as I do living here; but at least on earth, people's problems meant something! There was the potential for answers besides just answering to a talking box!"

"You dare speak of the LORD in such a manner!?" I recognized the hoarse voice of Stewart, the fifth elder, blurting out from off behind me.

"No, not the computer, I mean of all of you!" I raised my voice by multiple octaves, "The only reason any of you have the authority you do is just because you insist a talking box said so! None of you would even just go ahead and banish me from here without asking the machine first!"

"*I am not appreciative of this-*" As the LORD began his statement, his voice became drowned out by a snarling growl, then I was abruptly tackled from behind and thrown to the ground. Stewart had thrown himself on top of me and began pounding the back of my head, his hot breath blew angrily into my ear.

"MAKE A MOCKERY OF OUR SOCIETY, WILL YOU?!

AFTER ALL I'VE DONE?!" He screamed out, "I SAVED YOU, YOU UNGRATEFUL URCHIN!"

"*Fifth elder, you will cease this madness immediately! Someone remove him from atop the heretic!*" The LORD ordered, two other high council members came up and pulled the pulsating councilman off the ground, "*Clearly there has not been done a official evaluation in enough time. Send these two to the barracks for realignment to the path!*"

"Both?!" First Elder Questioned, "Milord, If I may, would it not be more appropriate only to banish the heretic to earth? Submitting a councilman of such high prestige would be... improper for an establishment as esteemed as ours..."

"*Hold to your oath elder, that all children of the Lord are equal in connection to the light, none may turn away or be turned away where they would otherwise be saved..*"

"Milord, I- we... would you not also agree that in this circumstance, that doctrine wouldn't be appropriate?" The First Elder asked.

"*Councilman, are you requesting that I disregard my divine objective to uphold the universal creed that guides the survival of humanity?*"

"No, no LORD, but- well, we the council conceived of and agreed on the terms of the creed, so would it not be prudent if we were influential in it's execution?"

"Oh?! What's that?! Computer problems?! Your god isn't responding properly?!" I snidely interjected, "Past its warranty maybe? Try sending a complaint to the producer?"

"That's enough out of you!" The first elder shouted, "You WILL be banished if not subjected to a worse punishment!"

"See! No more pretending! Why shop for deity parts online when you can just act like one yourself!" I could practically hear my blood pulsing through my veins as I shouted, "Let's admit it: You all wanted a deity that would give you authority over humanity, so you just built one!"

"This disrespect has gone far enough!" The first elder shouted, "Arrange to have him executed live over the colony's broadcast!"

"*SILENCE! ALL OF YOU!*" A sudden rumbling made everyone in the room direct their attention back to the LORD in the center of the room, "*It is clear from the display of malice here that there is a venom spreading in the hearts of my followers that will need to be treated! Therefore, it is my command that all colonies will return to earth and a grand reeducation will commence to ensure absolute commitment to the creed of the LORD of the universe!*"

"Wait-wait, milord! Do you not think you're being too hasty!" The first elder pleaded,

"He's already activated the colony's engines!" Another high councillor shouted, "Summon the engineers, he'll need to be rebooted again!"

"Save it!" I shouted, "This has been a long time coming!" In that moment of chaos, I grabbed hold of one of the high councillors that had wrestled Stewart off of me. With all my might, I heaved him

The God Complex
by Chandler Christie

over my shoulder and sent him hurtling towards the Lord of All's console, his head crashed through the screen of the computer and sent sparks flying high throughout the room. I then grabbed the spark shooter I had concealed in the lip of my boot and fired a bolt of sparkling energy into the cracked hole in the face of the Lord. A sparking, sizzling noise filled the air, accompanied by the smell of smoke. All the high councillors stood in numb silence.

"Sooo, can I go now?" I asked,

"You fool! Don't you see what you've done?!"

"So I broke your computer, just build another one!"

"Call as many engineers and technicians to this location as possible! We can possibly reconstruct LORD before it's too late!"

"What do you mean too late?" I asked.

At that moment, all the lights went out, and the air suddenly grew very thin. The rumbling sensation grew louder and more violent as it seemed like the air was heating up.

A Cold, Undercooked Goose
by Corbyn Andre

The flashing anger of the night burst forth, startling the horses that dragged my coach through the muddying road. My first glimpse of that dread house was through the viscous rain sliming the small window. The sleet-bound weather had little to do with the shudder that quaked me as I saw the estate's slate roof, and anachronistic Greek columns. Empty windows presided over a wild lawn that reminded me of some far off, exotic marshland.

My driver brought his horses to an anxious stop before the English oak door; the beasts nodding and snorting as I struggled out of the carriage, and shuffled toward the coachman—whose name fluttered from my mind—my boots slapped the mud, I pulled my coat tight to my body. The horses—the same colour as the flickering clouds above—shook their heads and their dark eyes trembled as I approached. The driver looked down at me, a friendly smile under his top hat. I handed him the previously shaken upon one pound and ten shillings.

"Pick up is at eleven tomorrow, and please," I paused to stare at the family crest haunting above the door; an oak leaf clamped in a crow's beak. "Don't be late," I shouted, competing with the requiem of the rain.

A Cold, Undercooked Goose
by Corbyn Andre

"Oh, aye, I shall have thee back t' train station at yer pleasure." He smiled and pinched the rim of his hat. I bid him a wordless goodbye. He lashed the horses and for a moment they snapped out of their anxiety, the fear of the incorporeal heavens replaced by the very real coachman's whip.

I battered the door with my fists since the ring of the cast iron knocker lay at my feet, its leonine head gasped at me with morbid shock. I waited in the rain, turning round to the oak forest at the end of the estate's boundaries. I lost myself to those trees, gnarled by the winter season. I used to watch the leaves float to the ground, stomping and crunching out of earshot of the house. As winter established itself, I would look out the windows and wait for the acorns and foxes to return. The frosted glass chilled me until my mother pulled me away and plopped me in front of the fireplace, beside my father's chair. He would be hidden by the tall back and arms of that cushioned throne, I would smell the tobacco, a spectre of my father. When he wasn't in that chair, I could lean against the arm and inhale fumes trapped in the fabric.

I did not hear the door open, but I knew it had. Perhaps it was the reek of tobacco or something more immaterial, yet I turned as if someone was there. I expected a butler and was unpleasantly surprised to see my father answering his own door. I hoped to have the few minutes between the entryway and the back parlour to try and shake off any last-minute dread.

"Hello, son."

"Hello, father."

A Cold, Undercooked Goose
by Corbyn Andre

He turned round and limped away, stabbing the ground with that silver crow-headed cane. The sharp clacking echoed throughout the house with no answer to the hollow caw.

"Your room's still there," my father said without turning. "Dinner will be soon, so get changed."

I didn't need to answer him, he knew I heard him, and he knew I would obey his direction. My father ambled past the stairs and into the kitchen. That had to have been the first time I saw him enter a kitchen. I noticed now that the house was in an oppressive gloom, none of the gas lamps or the candelabras were lit and I blinked, willing my eyes to adjust.

I ascended the stairs, each board gasping with the steps of my rain-heavy boots. On the middle landing I faced the seven-foot clock. As old as the house itself, and I used to believe it was as old as the Normans we trace our name to. Every hour of each day that diligent, wooden servant would cry out, filling me with mental anguish at the fifty-ninth minute of every hour. Every hour. Not to mention the pendulum itself that, with each swing, mocked the striking of my father's cane on the floor. It was stationed in the very middle of the house so, like a leech latched to the brain, inescapable no matter where one tried to crawl away. I stood face to face with the clock, silent now. Hushed by the perforation of several holes in its glass visage—all about the same size as the polished beak of that crow-headed cane.

A Cold, Undercooked Goose
by Corbyn Andre

After exactly a half hour, I descended the stairs and made my way to the family dining room. I grasped the dim-brass doorknob, freezing to the touch. My dinner jacket was designed for lively and well-heated social gatherings, so I tightened my cravat and hugged my collars as close to my neck as possible. I opened the door, greeted by light that hadn't been ordained by the storm. Dishes of food surrounded a single candelabra on the intimate table. This room was for family only, the actual dining hall sat directly opposite the lobby — empty since I was a boy.

My father hobbled in from the kitchens carrying a bottle of brandy. "Sit down, son. Plenty to eat."

I took my assigned seat, the one I *always* sat in. Always. To the left of my father and opposite my sister, well, her portrait. It hung behind and above her chair. Her pale, smiling face complimenting a pink dress, devoid of any brightness that pink suggested. A polite, stiff overlap of her hands, the confluence of her elbow-length white gloves; Lydia encased forever.

I barely recognized my sister, now bronzed by the incalescent Gibraltar sun; filled out by motherhood and mediterranean food. She was happy now, but I know the breeze of melancholy would chill her skin when she asked about this visit in her letters. Same as last year, and I daresay it will happen again next year. I would tell her about the storm and the holes in the clock. She would tell me about her husband's shore leave from the navy, how the first thing he did was grab their two small children and haul them to the beach for ginger beer.

A Cold, Undercooked Goose
by Corbyn Andre

His love strengthened by time and oceans. I believed her letters, despite my envy, that he was a good husband and father with a promised future in the navy. We had that honesty between us, one of the many lessons we learned from our father; only because when he told us he would give us a good crowing, we believed him.

Whilst I was remembering her, my father had sliced into a roast goose. He wielded a huge knife with the crude brutality of a man who had no idea what he was doing. He sat down after hacking the breast into pieces that approximated slices. I looked at the rest of the dishes, noticing the parsnips with grungy splotches, brussels sprouts emanating an odour unpleasant, and the carrots with dark red splatters. My father shoved a plate of the goose over to me with a lightly bandaged hand.

"Merry Christmas." From the deep, deep depths he conjured a memory of affability. His smile a phantom, I couldn't tell what it was, but it was unnatural, possessing only the spirit of being human. And then, it vanished in an instant.

"Merry Christmas, father."

"Where's the wife then?"

I cut a biteable piece of my goose. "Unfortunately, Sarah is a little under the weather, nothing to worry about. She's got the fire going, but wasn't feeling up to the travel," I lied.

My father listened with intention. His resting face, a glare at me. "It's tradition for family to be together on Christmas." I knew this blunt reply to be a command, and he would expect my wife to be here next year. However, she won't be, not anymore.

A Cold, Undercooked Goose
by Corbyn Andre

I lifted the fork to my mouth, only then I registered the scarlet mass in the middle of the goose. I put the food down.

"Who cooked this?"

"I did." He scoffed a piece of goose and chewed, scowling again at me. Regardless of how many times I saw it, I could never know if his face was simply at rest or a blast furnace for his anger.

The window that looked to the west lawn frosted over, ice spreading like a plague as sleet battered the glazing, the desolation of winter seeping into the house. I tried to ignore the cold, a ghast of my breath floated over my dinner plate.

"You did? Well, what happened to—Martha? Margaret?" I inspected the pinkness of the goose with my fork.

"Workshy Fenian." That was my father's code for mistreated beyond her limits.

"How long ago was that?"

"I don't know. Several months now."

"And no one has been here since?"

"Aye. But I gave him the boot too." I was not surprised. All my years in this house, I saw an endless rotation of butlers, drivers, footmen, cooks, gardeners, chambermaids, and all manner of guests driven from these premises by the slash of his cane or the splash of his spit.

After another bite, followed by a reluctant swallow, my father turned to me.

A Cold, Undercooked Goose
by Corbyn Andre

"Nothing wrong with the food. Eat up. I know some of you in that London eat those Yankee-doodle turkeys these days. Goose was good enough for us fifty years ago, it's good enough for us now. No sense breaking tradition just because you can."

"Father, we shouldn't be eating this. It's not cooked right." I knew better than to talk back, but I wasn't going to eat raw poultry.

"My word not good enough?" His face did not physically change but now I could feel it. A burst of thunder above us, the single candelabra dimmed by an explosion of lightning. It was almost imperceptible, but my father flinched. He rubbed where his horse crushed his knee as it fell in Crimea. He snatched the decanter of brandy that was to his right—within his exclusive reach—and ripped the stopper off. Caramel liquid sloshed into the glass, as well as on the table.

"Apologies father, but the goose is still a bit raw in the middle. I can go cook us something." I looked at the platter the rest of the goose laid on. Blood and juice congealed on the silver, as though entombed with its treasure.

"Nonsense." He scooped a handful of brussels with his bare hands and slammed them onto his plate. "What are you going to cook? We have goose at Christmas, and this is the only one I have."

"We can't eat this. Perhaps I can put it in the oven for a bit longer."

"What do you know about kitchens? You've never stepped foot beyond that door," he pointed behind him. "Let alone, know how to light an oven."

A Cold, Undercooked Goose
by Corbyn Andre

"I'm sure I can figure it out, Sarah's been teaching me how to cook."

"To cook? What on earth for?"

"Sometimes we cook together. Or if she's busy with letters or engaged at tea, I will make a simple pie for my supper." I knew this was the wrong answer but at this point the crucible had already spewed over.

"Oh, aye? No wonder she's ill. Not busy enough I tell you." He threw back his brandy, a loud gasp of what I knew to be my father's version of satisfaction followed. "That's the thing about these *petticoats*. You let that wife of yours think she can neglect one of her *simple* duties and it'll all be down hill. You purchased the house, you work for the house, but she'll own it. Mark me."

My eyes flickered to the chair to my left. My mother's seat. Behind and above her seat too was a portrait. She had a slight, elegant smile and her hair was straight, close to her head, ending in curls. She reminded me of a young portrait of Her Majesty I had seen a few times. My mother was young in the portrait, a version of her I never knew. She was always lively when playing with Lydia and I, but I always perceived the exhaustion on her face; strands of hair sticking out, the way she almost stumbled when it was cold outside. Lydia and our mother were only permitted to eat small morsels. Mother sat at this table with her wine, like a tiny hummingbird sustained by sweet nectar. She loved being near the fire in the cold evenings, and I could feel it radiate off her as well. My mother had a warm smile that the portrait above couldn't capture.

A Cold, Undercooked Goose
by Corbyn Andre

My father was about to continue but another barrage of thunder and lightning interrupted him, his brandy threatened to escape his crystal as he shook. For a final word on the matter, my father looked up at me, accentuating his words with his fork as he also did with his pipe or cane, "Christmas foods are supposed to be ate on Christmas." And he went back to his dinner.

I pushed at my food. My father glared at my plate, raising his fork to give me another lecture. "You were like your mother's parasol, you were, always at her bloody side. If you'd fit, you would've replaced her hat." I looked up at her. I pushed on the table, attempting to leave, yet to rise. He continued punctuating with his fork. Pointing. Jabbing. So close to my face. Pointing. Jabbing. I flinched and blinked with every thrust. I wanted to—

"I thought the cavalry would have straightened you out, as it did me, and my father, and his father, and his, going all the way—" He stopped. I looked down, he was sweating, retching. He turned his head to his side and vomited on the floor.

"Father? Are you—"

He vomited again. He struggled to breathe. He tried to loosen his cravat, but he couldn't find the knot. I rushed over, reaching for his neck, he swatted me away. I backed off, but lunged again to help. He grabbed the cane at his side and swiped at me.

"Father! I'm trying to—"

He got his cravat loose and vomited again. Red. Lightning flashed outside.

A Cold, Undercooked Goose
by Corbyn Andre

My father crumbled to the floor. He panted and convulsed. A bellow of thunder drowned his pleading. Pleading. But I couldn't hear. I sank to my knees. I wanted to help, somehow. He needed medicine. Something. Lightning followed thunder. Did he have any medicine? Thunder followed lightning. What did he need? I grabbed the candelabra so I could see better. What was I looking for? I wasn't a doctor. I didn't know. I wasn't a doctor. The clock on the stairs chimed. Eleven times. Riming its clockwork song.

My father, slick with sweat, convulsed. The cane slashed with hectic intention. I kept my distance. He vomited. I didn't know what I could do. Lightning, lightning, lightning. The fury above us. He waved the crow about. The clock chimed. My mother beamed. The clock chimed. My sister broke free. I cowered and cried. Thunder, thunder, thunder. Oak trees coming to get me. A corvid squawk above us. The clock again. Tolling in the room now. *Someone shut it up!* But there was no one. My father stopped. A final swing of the cane, a final word. That silver crow-headed cane falling. Clattering on the floor. Inept, only a thing now.

Everything stopped.

The clock struck once more before falling silent again. The house empty, settled. I remained awhile, kneeling over my father. I hunched over the corpse until it turned as blue as the night. Sleet turned to silent snow, the worst of the storm moving on. I tried to sob, it was the appropriate thing to do.

A Cold, Undercooked Goose
by Corbyn Andre

Instead, I rose, blew out the candles, and collected the plates, dumping them all in the kitchen basin. I picked up my father's chair and pushed it back in, shoving my father's leg aside with my foot to put the chair in its proper place. Only myself, a dead clock, and a freezing butchered goose haunted this great house. I would send for the doctor tomorrow, he wouldn't make a call now, it was Christmas. And so, I retired to bed.

A Cold, Undercooked Goose
by Corbyn Andre

Art by Siena Stark

A Name is a Gift
by Myra Monday

A name is a gift
One everyone gets when they're young
Everyone uses it
It's expected of you
But what happens when it doesn't feel right?
When it feels thick on the tongue
Like sickly sweet molasses
Stuck in your mouth
The feeling of a scream
That will never come out
Wanting to run
But having doubt
Wanting to hide
But you know what they'll shout
Shout the name that lurches your heart
With the fleeting sense of security
Replaced with hurt
For what is a name
But letters to make sounds
That sound good in our ears
Something to be proud by when someone cheers
What is a name

A Name is a Gift
by Myra Monday

But a gift we were given

One expected we carry with us forever

The only gift meant to last

Never outgrow

The first gift

The longest gift

A connection to our past

But gifts don't always last forever

Well most of them don't

As we grow and change; gifts we once had loved

Now are only loved in our memories

But the first gift we do not choose

No say in, no influence

One everyone else will use

Before the person ever knows what to do

A part of themselves were chosen

A part you're not supposed to lose

Yet a name is a gift

And gifts change with time

A gift you get now

Won't be the same as when you were five

And while most names don't change

There are some people who know

That their first gift

A name

Is not one that will help them grow

A Name is a Gift
by Myra Monday

So why can't they change it to one they feel fits
For a name is a gift
And not all gifts fit

Heart of Stone
by Teresa Anderson

"How can you be so cold?" Ye-joon averted his eyes, glaring at the water. "I mean nothing to you?"

"Not nothing." I hugged my arms. "But not as much as you thought."

Ye-joon lowered his chin. "No, no, I don't—" he lifted his head. "Do you not trust me?"

"Of course, I do—"

"Then believe me," he said, collecting my hand. "I can convince your father to let me marry you."

I tore my eyes away from his face to the frayed threads on his collar. At first, his worn clothes had impressed me; now, they left me broken. "I need to go."

"Dan-bi, wait. Please."

I couldn't. Not if my cheeks were to remain dry.

"Tomorrow," he called after me. "I will be here again tomorrow."

At that, turning around was easy. The words that came were not. "I won't be."

Ye-joon stared. "So, you are ambitious, after all." I said nothing, and he shook his head as though no longer recognizing me. "What made you like stone?"

I could not voice the reason. To do so would give me away.

Heart of Stone
by Teresa Anderson

"Goodbye, Ye-joon."

Alone in my room, I retrieved the torn strips of a faded blue sash from my cabinet. The sash had belonged to Ye-joon, and he'd reduced it to bandages after I'd rolled my ankle. It was how I met him. But I had seen him before that.

The edges of my eyes stung. I kept my word, and two weeks had passed since.

Eager footsteps padded down the hall, and I shoved the sash into its hiding spot.

"Your father just came home with the most wonderful news—why are you crying?" Mother lowered to her knees, meeting me on the floor. "It will be all right. You do not need to fret over Kim Woo-seok any longer."

Ah, yes, him. The match Father had arranged. No one knew that I had intentionally spilled tea on Woo-seok's lap. No one knew that I had sabotaged the match before him, too. No one, except Ye-joon.

I sniffled, grateful to have a misdirection. "But his father—"

"Do not worry about the Taxation Minister. Soon, your father will be promoted above him." Mother could hardly contain her excitement. "There will be a selection. You are going to be a royal concubine," she said with a proud wiggle of her brow.

My mouth slipped open; a sour hole scorched my gut. "They won't choose me," I managed because my refusing was illegal.

Heart of Stone
by Teresa Anderson

A tsk. "Of course, they will. This bout of jittery fingers will pass," she said, tapping my hand. "You will impress them. So, get some rest, Dan-bi. You cannot have puffy eyes for the first inspection."

She rushed out as quickly as she came, and I couldn't move.

I didn't have her disposition to endure. To turn a blind eye when Father visited his concubine, or when he spent the night at a gisaeng house. She could stomach a loveless marriage, while I could never. But that was all Father would permit me.

And that morning, when he prepared our genealogical background for the palace's review, I glared at his spine.

I glared at the reason I had become stone.

"Remember, demure..." Mother trailed off, noticing the perfume pouch, my *norigae*, hanging from my jacket ribbon. "Where did you get this?"

Ye-joon.

"From you," I said. "You must have forgotten."

Her frown deepened. The norigae was not as fancy as my others. No time was given for her to order a replacement, though, because in strolled members of the palace.

I was disappointed, but not surprised when they proclaimed my advancement. My face and figure were condemning. But I would be patient.

Once free, the pond would be my first destination.

Maybe Ye-joon was still visiting there, still waiting. I deserved

Heart of Stone
by Teresa Anderson

none of his effort, but that determination of his was all that occupied my mind as I rode in the palanquin. More so, as I saw a beggar in the street. That man had the same gaunt face as the one Ye-joon had bought a meal for.

I curled into myself.

Before he'd helped me, before he'd flashed me a disarming smile and bandaged my sprain, I'd witnessed his heart. For it wasn't only a meal that Ye-joon offered, but an attentive ear and a warm bed at an inn. I'd watched as the innkeeper escorted the beggar to his room, and Ye-joon, he'd remained at the table, alone, scowling as though frustrated.

I had recognized that look. Often, I wore the same when I ran out of rice balls to give to orphans. The disease was a corrupt system, and rare moments of kindness were an insufficient treatment.

Still, Ye-joon, who was too poor for my parents to accept, had tried to make a difference.

"Don't give up on me," I whispered into the stuffy palanquin. "Please, wait."

Inspections, all day, even during some nights. But, it didn't matter that I laughed inappropriately, broke cups, tossed and turned, snored, hacked and coughed. Nor did it matter when I tripped on the stairs, ruined my sleeves with ink, or stained my embroideries with smears of blood from needle pricks.

Father must have bribed someone.

Heart of Stone
by Teresa Anderson

We all stood in a row of matching hanboks, but we were permitted one piece of individuality. I wore the norigae, as I had every day since my being confined to these walls. Today was our interview, a series of complex questions to glean the state of our mind. I was next, and I rubbed my eyes to make them puffier and more shadowed.

"Look," squealed a girl at the end of the row. "There he is!"

Curiosity got the better of me, but I failed to lower my hands in time. All I saw was the King's black silk, two-tiered crown, his ikseongwan, and the golden dragons decorating his shoulders on his bright red robe, his hongryongpo. Twin rows of guards, eunuchs, and maids trailed behind him. He was tall, like Ye-joon, and I turned away, as the other girls gushed and giggled.

"I heard he prefers books to women," said one girl. "Always reading, and he hates to be bothered. I heard he didn't even want a selection."

The girl next to me let her shoulders sag. "Perhaps there's a court maid he would rather favour."

"Forget the maids and the books," ordered Hong Ma-ri. My greatest rival, according to Mother. "Once he sees us, he'll pay them no mind. Excluding Dan-bi, of course." Her mouth curled as she faced me. "Upset stomach again?"

The other girls grimaced, all reminded of the loud fart I had unleashed yesterday. That, alone, should have sent me home. Yet, here I was.

Ma-ri did not wait for my response. "You're a disgrace," she said. "A sloppy, disgusting disgrace. Your father will have to settle for a commoner as a son-in-law."

Yes, he would.

I feigned a yawn, ignored the additional ridicule, and stared at the ground. Kicking my foot to dust my slippers, a pebble caught my eye. Dipped and curved at the top to make twin arches, and slightly pointed at the bottom.

The shape of a heart.

What made you like stone?

People like this.

These girls were no better than my father, greedy for a chance to elevate their station. Some planned to manipulate the King, encourage this law over that one. Why, just last night, I'd overheard Ma-ri trying to convince other girls that the King's plan to widen entry for state examinations shouldn't succeed.

Filthy peasants cannot be allowed government positions, she'd warned.

But wouldn't such a possibility reduce the level of poverty and hunger?

For a fleeting moment, I thought I should be a concubine. His reign was young, yet if this king was good, if he did care about the state of his people, then I would offer encouragement, not corruption.

My name was called, and I bent to retrieve the stone, dismissing the thought.

No. I would not be chosen. I would go home.

Heart of Stone
by Teresa Anderson

Glaring at the puddle in the courtyard, I wanted to splash myself with mud. I had planned to act flippant and dumb during my interview, but my mind had been on Ye-joon. I answered each question like I was speaking to him, echoing our conversations about how Joseon should be. Kinder, equal. At the time, the ministers didn't seem impressed, and I was convinced I'd won.

Wrong.

Ma-ri had also advanced to the final round. She and the second candidate were equally appalled by my inclusion. Ma-ri was so furious, in fact, that she'd slapped me last night.

How much did your father bribe? she'd demanded.

My cheek burned, and I had stayed silent, for I stopped believing Father could have buffered my sabotage so thoroughly. He wasn't that wealthy, nor that persuasive.

Not that he was worth speculating on. Today, once the three of us were seated in front of the King, I would become my sloppiest, my most disgusting.

The head eunuch came down the steps, and I did not bother to square my shoulders.

"His Highness has decided," the eunuch said, and we all froze. The King hadn't met any of us yet, that was the purpose of this last round. "Seo Dan-bi. Follow me, His Highness waits for you."

My eyes widened; Ma-ri let out a wail. She tried to yank my plait, but I was already backing away.

I broke into a run. The guards at the gate were too shocked at my fleeing to stop me. Shouting, from the head eunuch and others, but all I heard was Ye-joon, begging me to wait, like he had at the pond.

That water, his reflection in it was all I saw, and I refused to let him become nothing more than that. I refused to let him become lost, forever haunting me.

Faster I ran, tears streaming down my face.

But I was ignorant of the palace layout. Meeting a dead-end, I turned in desperation and came to a halt.

Rushing footsteps neared, accompanied by the flash of a red robe, and I dropped to my knees, my forehead hovering above the ground. The King, himself, had chased me, and he, alone, had caught up to me.

I trembled, for I had disobeyed to the extreme, and my punishment would stretch to both parents.

Still, I could not hold my tongue. "Please, Your Highness. I have someone at home."

The King caught his breath, swallowed, then, "You love him?"

Stunned, my tears stalled, and I lifted my head.

No, no, I must be exhausted. I hadn't slept, or maybe Ma-ri had poisoned me, or maybe—

He lowered to his knees in front of me, and I couldn't deny it any longer.

"I wanted to tell you," he said, "but not before I knew that it was me you loved, and not..." he trailed off, waving at the golden dragon on his chest. "Do you?" he asked, his eyes pinned to my norigae.

Ye-joon—was that even his real name? But it was all I knew him by. Here, royalty only went by title.

Somehow, I found my voice. "What if I can't give you sons?" That had been Mother's fate; one of the reasons Father sought other women. And heirs would be the most important here.

"You are all I want." Ye-joon shifted on his knees, coming a bit closer. "Joseon can be better, and we can achieve that, together, but I will not force you to be with me." Ye-joon's hand lifted, almost reaching for mine, but he stopped himself. "So, one last time. Do you want to be my family and be at my side?"

Part of me was a little disappointed. Instead of my forbidden elopement, Father would get what he wanted.

But so would I.

My fingers tore into my norigae's pouch and retrieved the stone.

A slow smile stretched across Ye-joon's face, and grew wider when he closed his hand around the stone, warming its heart shape. He knew my answer, he must have known it when he saw me wearing the norigae upon entering the palace, but I said it anyway.

As I should have done when he first asked me.

"Yes," I said. "Always."

Then, he kissed me, held me, and I was finally home.

The Witches Who Burned
by Bailey J. Wilson

300 years ago
witches watched their sisters burn
women were forced into submission
and coven after coven faced eradication
when all they did was dare to speak
dare to think
dare to breathe

The witches who survived
learned to keep their craft hidden
keep their heads down
keep their mouths shut

they watched as *"Witch"* became synonymous with *"Evil"*
as *"Woman"* became synonymous with *"Less"*
as *"Different"* became synonymous with *"Dead"*

And like shoes and shirts that are outgrown
their trade and trauma was passed down,
mother to daughter
with a beginner's lesson in never being too loud
never standing out

The Witches Who Burned
by Bailey J. Wilson

never trying too hard

Their *other* was kept behind closed doors
whispered in clandestine meetings
sharing spells in tiny notes
that were set ablaze after reading
lest they be seen by the malicious male gaze

But one day,
the witches of the world
remembered that in the days of olde
we gathered in covens
danced around pyres in forests
with the kind of reckless abandon
that only comes in a space full of women

we made feasts of men's tyranny
and dined like Queens on the lies we were fed
we were loud and wild,
we were strong and free,
and we were one
because together we knew
we were more powerful than any patriarch

So we exchanged our redwood wands for protest pickets
and marched with hat pins and hands in pockets

The Witches Who Burned
by Bailey J. Wilson

that the world did not want us to have

Together again, we would not be silenced
and the men who once burned us alive
conceded victory in public
but plotted their revenge
within their boardroom walls
creating manic pixie girls,
and ditzy blondes
to reinforce the ideas
They wanted us to be

The words changed
but the messages stayed the same:
witches are *evil*
women are *less*
different is *dead*
They say it now through magazines
with back-handed compliments
and photoshopped beauty standards
They learned from our last encounter
and started turning sister against sister

When we started getting wiser
to the voices they were stealing
They took away our rights

The Witches Who Burned
by Bailey J. Wilson

forcing women to be what They wanted:
a cauldron for Their own potion of patriarchy,
a vessel to create more of *Them*

more boys to fill with preconceived notions
of what it means to be a man
and more girls to keep locked in ivory towers
used only for their beauty and never their brains

But how long can you keep us docile?
We have fire flowing through our veins
and blood between our legs
just because you cannot see the rebellion brewing
doesn't mean it's not about to boil over
our feminine rage has reached its peak
and here at the summit, we will make our stand

We will not let our bodies become government property.
We will not let you train our daughters to be obedient dolls.
We will not let our voices become background noise to ignore.
We will not let you drown our dreams in the water of your whims.

We have fashioned our fingertips into flint
and all it would take is one strike
to set the whole world ablaze
to burn you alive

The Witches Who Burned
by Bailey J. Wilson

like we once did
and wouldn't that just be
A genuine piece
of poetic justice.

BLOODWRITING
by Brennan Kenneth Brown

An Excerpt from *HOW THE ENGLISH DEGREE WILL SAVE THE WORLD: Queering, Decolonizing and Democratizing Literary Studies for Generation Z*

In the hallways of Mount Royal University's English department, the reckoning is no different than at any other school: I peoplewatch faces bathed in the blue light of phones in fluorescent-lit hallways. Thumbs moving with the mechanical precision of assembly line workers. Each swipe lasts exactly 15 seconds before the next dopamine hit. Even in literature seminars where we're meant to be discussing Chaucer or Whitman, students are simultaneously consuming and creating narratives across multiple platforms—laptops display split screens dressed half academic paper, half Netflix. Between classes I walk around campus and watch students congregate around the few outlets in the older buildings like pilgrims at a shrine. The very concept of "text" has exploded into a thousand strange forms: fifteen-second video essays cutting deeper for students than any academic paper, sprawling collaborative fanfictions where readers and writers blur together in real-time, memetic satires of corporate mascots, roleplay forums where teenagers craft elaborate mythologies through nothing but status updates. Dozens of literary forms being born and dying every day. The boundaries between creator and consumer, between high art and shitpost, between canon and transformation, all seem to be dissolving in real-time, surely. Salt in hot water.

The East Gate Starbucks is my favourite observation point. From here, I can see the parade of devices carried as external organs. Where traditional literature kept author and reader at arm's length, separated by publishers and professors, they're now messaging each other fanart at 3am, building sprawling narrative together in Google Docs, turning screenshots into web weaving, crafting theories in nested reply threads stretching toward infinity. Thousands of social media posts and messages pass through our bodies every second. Ghost signals passing through my bones as radiation.

When I pass through the Riddell Library's spiral doors, I think about how the Internet was supposed to be our Library of Alexandria—infinite, democratic, eternal. Instead, it is perceived as the carnival of infinite distractions. The sacred space of literary study seems increasingly profaned by everything all of the time. The careful consideration of text replaced by the ephemeral.

The tension within our English classrooms runs deeper than a simple generational divide or arbitrary technological barrier. Here, faculty are still steeped in centuries of literary tradition—in practices of close reading, theoretical analysis, and careful citation—and do not know how to interface with students who have developed an entirely different way of engaging with text. These students navigate complex networks of meaning through reblogs and recommendations, crafting interpretative frameworks through what can be argued as collaborative annotation and remix. Neither way of reading is inherently superior, yet their seeming incompatibility threatens to fracture the very foundation of literary studies moving forward.

As both scholar and digital native, I find myself straddling worlds—moving between traditional academic spaces and the misunderstood digital landscapes where contemporary literature increasingly lives and breathes. On Tuesday afternoon I'm sitting in my usual spot in the library when I notice a student switching rapidly between tabs—one with their assigned Joyce reading, another with a YouTube video essay about *Ulysses,* and a third showing a Reddit thread debating interpretations of the text. They're not "just reading" anymore but participating in multiple simultaneous conversations about meaning. Every few minutes they pause to type something, contributing their own voice to this brave new world of literary discussion. The air feels different.

I'm reminded of an old GeoCities archive on one of the mechanical hard drives I used back in high school. While these sites are regarded only as amateur creations—they were the first flowering of truly democratic digital literature. Anyone could share anything with anyone. Effortlessly. Free. Buried among the animated GIFs and comic sans were blog posts from the late 90s—raw, sometimes-bizarre thoughts from people who weren't trying to build personal brands or monetize existence. I'm reminded of *Justin's Links from the Underground,* one of the earliest personal websites launched in 1994 by Justin Hall. While early websites like his are now often dismissed as amateur, they were among the first flowering of truly democratic digital literature. Anyone could share anything with anyone. Effortlessly. Free. Justin chronicled his life in intimate detail—his thoughts, relationships, struggles—long before the term "blog" even existed. In an interview, he said that "[t]he best use of our technology enhances our humanity. It lets us shape our narrative and share our story and connect us." This is digital literature's transformative power—the ability to create spaces where traditional barriers to literary production fall away. I think of the sacredness wrapped in HTML. Ceremony disguised as content. Each post is both a therapy session and proof of existence. A seed planted in soil that might one day grow into something more. I am a child of the Internet's Wild West, witness to the revolution in who gets to create and define literature, born on the cusp between Millennial and Generation Z—too young for LiveJournal, too old for TikTok. I watched sites and communities like GeoCities rise and fall like Atlantis, always standing at the shore, words caught in my throat, believing I had nothing worth saying.

It wasn't until I became a cook at a children's hospice that I finally began to write publicly. Death has a way of loosening one's grip on perfectionism. My first posts on *Medium.com* emerged like careful footprints in fresh snow, each title a small rebellion against God:

- *Death Writing: Meaningless Ideas, Timeless Work*
- *The Art of Losing: How lucky it is to not be victorious*
- *Dying Without Seeing You Again: Living on fire without putting yourself out—and cherishing the heat*

The democratization of digital platforms meant there is no

BLOODWRITING
by Brennan Kenneth Brown

institutional permission needed to add your voice to the conversation. For almost a decade, I crafted these small testaments to existence. Each piece was a stone added to a cairn, marking a path through the wilderness. But now even *Medium*, that last outpost of thoughtful digital writing, feels like an independent bookstore on clearance sale in a dilapidated, liminal mall. Yet this too is part of digital literature's nature—platforms rise and fall, but the impulse to create persists, finding new forms and spaces.

Digital platforms enable new forms of writing and reading—and in that, demand new forms of pedagogy. I once learned about winter counts—pictographic histories painted on buffalo hide, each image representing one year's most significant event. Like those Indigenous historians, today's digital natives are creating their own ways of recording and sharing knowledge, ways that often go unrecognized by traditional academic structures. I think about each essay, poem, post as a digital winter count. Each title a pictograph, each paper a hide stretched and worked until it becomes usable, becomes art.

The revelation transforms my understanding of what the English degree must become: For we are not watching the death of literacy; we're watching its mutation. In the 4th floor of the university library, there's a climate-controlled room full of medieval artefacts—I think of hands cramping around quills, monks illuminated manuscripts, the slow accretion of human knowledge. Now, in the Tim Horton's line, I watch a student craft a perfectly worded Instagram caption, her thumbs flying over the glass screen with the same intensity those monks must have felt. These are, in fact, parallel acts of literary creation, both deserve serious study and consideration within our discipline. The English degree must evolve to embrace these new forms of meaning-making.

This isn't about white-knuckling our way to continue getting funding and enrollment. No, it's about recognizing how digital natives naturally blur boundaries between consumption and creation, between academic and creative. I found this out during a Write Club meeting last semester. As we were packing up, someone mentioned they were running late for a D&D session. "Oh, I write the campaign," they said casually, as though that wasn't hundreds of pages of world-building and character arcs over months or years. When I asked to see some of it, they hesitated—never considering it "real" writing before. There are so many of these secret writers, it seems. Finding our own ways to practice bloodwriting.

***

Bloodwriting begins with a pulse. The thrum of your fingers against keys. Flutters in your chest when you press publish. A quiet conviction that your words—whether they take the form of a scholarly essay or a thread on BlueSky or Threads or Mastodon—deserve to exist in the world. It's not craft or talent or clout. Bloodwriting is the courage to leave a mark, to say: Hi, I am here, I think, I feel, I exist.

The democratization of literary creation demands we reconceptualize what counts as "reading" and "writing" within the academy. For the surprise isn't that people are reading less; it's that they're reading differently. Between classes, I start noticing the secret

BLOODWRITING
by Brennan Kenneth Brown

readers: the maintenance worker listening to an audiobook while changing air filters, the cafeteria cashier reading webnovels on her phone, the security guard who turns out to be working on dissertation on break. The university itself becomes a text, layered with narratives that challenge traditional notions of literary study. Feminist and Queer scholar Gloria Anzaldúa asked "why am I compelled to write?... Because the world I create in the writing compensates for what the real world does not give me" (168). This compensation now happens through digital means, as marginalized voices find platforms that traditional publishing and academia long denied them. Bloodwriting is the act of creation and compensation, but it's also an act of connection. Every word you write publicly and digitally begins a thread—invisible but real—connecting you to others who resonate with your truth. These threads weave a different kind of web, one that exists beyond the commercial internet—a web of human voices speaking their truth in messy, glorious complexity.

The English degree of the future must recognize these new forms of literary connection and creation. When our ancestors painted on cave walls, they mixed their own blood with the ochre to make the images more powerful (Bunney). More alive. Everything that matters costs us something of ourselves. Every time you open a blank document, post a thread, share a story online, you're creating a small altar to possibility.

In the margins of traditional academia, these new literary forms flourish. Walking past the Milky Way room late one evening, a peer shows me fanfiction they wrote about their favorite video game characters with Queer headcanons. They'd posted it at 3AM, exhausted after finishing a term paper, but this was the writing that felt urgent—that needed to come out. By morning it had dozens of comments from readers. Not peer-reviewed, not properly cited, but alive with the pulse of real connection. These are the texts our students are creating and consuming, the literature that matters to their lives. Our pedagogy must evolve to embrace them.

The term "digital native" suggests we were born knowing how to navigate this landscape of screens and signals. But what we really inherit is something much older: the need to make marks that matter. We are all trying to prove we were here, we lived, we had something to say. The English degree must become a space where all forms of literary meaning-making are valued, where digital and traditional texts speak to each other in productive dialogue. Poet and essayist Adrienne Rich called writing "re-vision—the act of looking back, of seeing with fresh eyes, of entering an old text from a new critical direction" (18). Bloodwriting is this re-vision for the digital age—entering our own lives from new directions, making and remaking ourselves explicitly in public, turning our wounds into windows.

Our challenge as scholars and teachers is to create an English degree that honors both tradition and transformation. During midterms last year, I discovered that the university's WiFi has a dead zone exactly three tables wide in the northwest corner of the old library—the one now being excavated for asbestos. Students avoided it like a curse, but I started sitting there intentionally. In this makeshift Faraday cage, a bubble of digital silence, my writing changes. It becomes more urgent, less concerned with performance. This too must be part of our pedagogy—understanding how different spaces, both digital and physical, shape literary creation.

The English degree of the 21st century must become a hybrid space where bloodwriting is possible. Audre Lorde reminds us that "poetry is not a luxury. It is a vital necessity of our existence." Neither is bloodwriting a luxury. It is survival. It is resistance. It is proof. It is the future of literary studies, if we have the courage to embrace it.

The semester edges toward winter. The days grow shorter, and the lights of phones and laptops burn brighter in the darkness. I recall in one of my literary theory lectures, I listened about how penny dreadfuls and serial novels—things we now study seriously—were accused of rotting young minds no different than TikTok.

To bloodwrite, you need only what you already have: your life, your truth, your device, your willing fingers. Every smartphone is a publishing house, every social media account an open letter. The democratization of voice that the early internet promised? It's still possible, one bloodwritten post at a time.

As we move deeper into the digital age, even our acts of resistance take on new forms. When the Luddites broke machines in the 19th century, they weren't against technology—they were against the dehumanization caused by technology. Bloodwriting is modern Luddism: not a rejection of digital tools, but a reclamation of them for deeply human purposes, for literary creation that matters.

Snow falls on campus, and the paths between buildings become treacherous. Students walk with their heads down, but now

BLOODWRITING
by Brennan Kenneth Brown

it's to watch for ice, not screens. In these moments of enforced awareness, I see them notice things: the way snow catches in the brutalist architecture, the steam rising from the heating vents, the tracks we leave behind that will be covered by fresh snow, only to be made again tomorrow.

This too is bloodwriting for the transformed English degree. The daily practice of paying attention, of making marks that matter, of insisting on depth in an age of surfaces. Stories are medicine. Bloodwriting carries this healing power into digital space. Every time you write your truth you're creating medicine. You're healing yourself, and you're leaving healing for others to find.

Sometimes, late at night in the library, when the screens around me flicker like stars, I think about those monks, wrinkled drunk hands cramping around quills, believing in the importance of making marks on paper. I think about my own hands on this keyboard, practicing this ancient human urge to record, to remember, to reach out across time and space and say: this matters, this matters, this matters. The English degree must become a space where all these forms of mattering can coexist and flourish. And sometimes, in the quiet moments between keystrokes, I swear I can hear them writing back.

I coined the term "bloodwriting" to describe how Indigenous ways of knowing—where story, memory, and identity flow together inseparably—is our relationship with modern digital literature. I call it bloodwriting because it is our DNA pressed into words—not content for algorithms, but fragments of our being encoded into digital spaces. In a world burning with crisis, bloodwriting teaches students that their voices *are* literature, that writing itself is an act of survival. The English classroom must become a space where this vital creation exists.

The English degree stands at a critical juncture. My position as a Queer Métis scholar, digital native, and member of Generation Z has shown me both the profound challenges and remarkable possibilities ahead. We must reconstruct the English degree not just to survive but to thrive as a vital force for social transformation. When we recognize that all forms of literary creation emerge from the same human need to leave marks that matter, we begin to see how digital spaces enhance rather than threaten traditional literary studies. The crisis facing the English degree is real, but so is the opportunity for radical reconstruction. Embracing digital lit, centering marginalized voices and democratizing access to literary expression, and understanding bloodwriting as both metaphor and methodology, we can forge an English degree capable of addressing our current moment of crisis. The work ahead is challenging, but the stakes—extreme polarization to democratic decay—demand nothing less than complete transformation. The future of the English degree lies in the creation of new, more inclusive spaces where all forms of literary meaning-making can flourish. In the end, this isn't about saving the English degree—it's about saving ourselves.

Part Two:
COMPANIONSHIP

The Ballad of Eve
by Spencer Heindle

Born to be inferior, but expected to be cheerier,
Eve gifts earth with life
A woman from a man, waiting under his hand,
the picture-perfect wife
Lived in a garden, but not without pardon,
Adam warns her not to take
Was obedient at first, but curiosity burns with thirst,
she curses that goddamn snake
A heavenly Father rules all, yet he lost sight of his doll,
and so she sneaks a little bite
That Father now mourns, his garden infested with thorns,
she gains unholy sight
Naked is Eve, and now so is he, their bodies are no longer pure
For its all her fault, womb drenched in salt, humanity begins in fear
Drats to her veil, her heart beats will fail,
a downfall the Father did not fathom
We suffer through her, a noose weaved with pearls,
fruitless offspring of Adam
I'm one of her daughters, sent off to the slaughter,
fingers pointed at me in rage
Birth brings here a soul, women shatter their whole,
she's useless in old age

The Ballad of Eve
by Spencer Heindle

Don't think ill of me, as if Eve bathes in fleas,
triad as a wicked witch
Eve is a mother, for girls damned and smoothed,
earth's exclusive bitch.

forever, unconditionally
by Spencer Heindle

I yearn for my blood to scorch like the sun.
I hallucinate being smothered by my suitor's love: unconditionally forever.

I imagine a man so suave Apollo falls to his feet,
My eyes conjure hearts within the webs of my dreams.

One day he appears outside my fantasy,
My breath stops dead as my heart beats happily.

My beating bosom inhales to fit one more,
Dense clouds partway for my desire to soar.

He settles with ease in the corner of my head,
And I lose track of the times I wake in his bed.

He stamps his claim in a smacking kiss,
I immortalize my lust through words of bliss.

A deep smoky whisper melts into steam,
while his calloused hands entice a pleasurable scene.

forever, unconditionally
by Spencer Heindle

Hops on a train- now he's off to a job,
And I panic over distances while choking on sobs.

Crumbling roads stretching out of my reach,
Passion commands me to cling like a leach.

His patience is soothing as my expectations dry out,
The reality of love leaves a sour taste in my mouth.

How can love flourish when miles apart?
He says love is a choice made by your heart.

The now lies in shadows of a doubtful mind,
But in memory we share devotion collected by time: unconditionally forever.

Anecdotes from a Hedonist
by Felix Da Costa Gomez

Growing up, my friends were assholes, so I never really had a solid idea of what companionship was. I shouldn't say all of my friends, really it was only the guys. I went to elementary school at a place called St. Benedict, just off of Southland drive. The playground was the best part, and it probably still is if the tire swings are still there. Across from the playground there's a massive soccer field and if you're standing on the metal stairs outside of the foyer, it looks like the fence sits at the horizon denying the sky of its freedom. I don't remember why, but I remember all of my first friends being girls. We would push each other on the tire swings and I would push too hard and Chloe would land on her knees in the rock bed of the playground and start crying and not speak to me for days. Getting hurt is part of the fun of growing up, memories basked in blood make for good jokes thirteen years later sitting in Boston Pizza, and Chloe enthusiastically tells my girlfriend that I used to tie my t-shirt into a bra to make the others laugh, so she and I are pretty even. So, let's recap. Grew up going to shitty catholic school because of my immigrant parents, hung out with the girls opposed to the boys, and my nickname growing up was Fifi. What's that? Oh yeah. Everyone thought I was gay. How'd you guess?

    By the time I turned eight, I realized I should probably start hanging out with the boys my age in an attempt to preserve my fragile masculinity. Word of advice; girls make better friends. That's not me being funny, they really do. I never understood this "girls are bitches" thing from other girls. I feel like a lot of the girls I knew growing up matured emotionally faster than the boys. By the time we turned ten they were already resolving their issues with conversations. One time when I was ten, my friend Jack made me so mad that I slammed his face in with my metal water bottle. His nose is a little crooked now. It's a shame, he would've been a handsome guy.

    The first boy I called my best friend was named Fred. We became friends after he saw that no one wanted to buddy up with me for the fourth grade science fair, so he asked me if I wanted to do it with him and I said sure. We didn't make it to the city wide competition, our project was too typical; dinosaur amber. We spent an entire month at his place working diligently on the circular dining table stapling plagiarized wikipedia entries and Jurassic Park still images to the surface of the trifold. After the science fair, I went to Fred's house every Tuesday. His house was a lot more fun than mine. His basement was decked out in bookshelves fostering complete lego sets and he had a punching bag and a gym facing the grand window displaying a picturesque backyard. There was a small cupboard-like space we used to record Youtube videos that had to be edited in rough cuts because his brother would barge in and shout slurs. There was another small closet under the stairs with bins full of superhero action figures and plastic lightsabers that broke way too fast and developed white bruises from the weight of our smacks.

Anecdotes from a Hedonist
by Felix Da Costa Gomez

Fred himself was a pretty cool guy. He always had a cheery smirk on his face that never broke no matter what happened to him. One time I threw a Teddy Graham at his neck and he started crying. His face was all red, tears dripping off of his crumpled chin as if he received the worst news of his little life, and then he went back to laughing a couple of seconds afterwards. The Teddy Graham incident was a rare occurrence though. In the ten years that I knew Fred, I never saw him cry again.

My house didn't come with the luxury of an XBox or a fast computer, so we would wrestle and he always won. I was exhausted, mouth prolapsed blowing exasperated hot breaths into his face and he picked my nose and made me eat the gunk. That boy was feral, he climbed the stairs on all fours beating his fists against the carpet like a gorilla and when he hit me it felt like a wooden baseball bat beating on the peaks of my ribs.

He was quick witted but had a problem with authority. He was homeschooled for the last part of fourth grade because the teacher had a personal vendetta against him, and Fred was smart enough to understand his situation.

"The biggest problem in his life is a nine year old," He would say. "What a pathetic life."

Throughout the rest of elementary school, junior high, and high school, I never left Fred's side. We were always seen on the playground together, throwing loose zippers at unsuspecting kids, watching them fall to the ground holding their necks and kicking up grass wondering what hit them. I went to his hockey games and afterwards we would go back to his house and binge Lord of the Rings. I never had anything but praise for him. I always made sure he knew how loved he was, how smart I thought he was, and that he was the toughest kid on the playground. Showered him in so much affection that the small boy I knew drowned and died in the bathtub and when his body rose to the surface of the water and his nose and eyes kissed air something demonic entered him and all I could do was watch as my best friend disappeared and cruelty incarnate took his place.

    After Junior High, he got a big head. I never humbled him so he grew up believing anything was possible for him, and the more I observed him the more that became true. He excelled in class when he wasn't smoking pot or getting caught in the back alley with a spliff, and he was the school's wrestling lead and a violent hockey player. Meanwhile, I became his idiot. I never stood up for myself so he believed I had no backbone, and everything I said was dismissed with an adamant "Felix, you're an idiot."

    He became selfish and got the attention of several people by putting on a kind face, but I knew him well enough to know that the smirk I once admired was a wicked charm that caged the poison of a ruthless tongue. I was replaced because I didn't agree with his opinions, and he got a new lap dog that kisses his ass more than I did. I spent most of my adolescence crawling back to Fred like an abused skinny dog that still comes at the call of his owner. Fred taught me that companionship takes the spirit of a dog. He taught me that companionship means to respect everybody but myself, and it's a code I've stuck closely to long after his absence.

Now, while Fred is a terrible person, he was still my friend. Most of the bad stuff we did together. We contemplated robbing a liquor store one time, but I bailed out. I watched him hype himself up in his cracked bathroom mirror buttoning up a black dress shirt and a face mask. When we turned sixteen, we exchanged midnight talks about the future for getting red eye stoned on his couch. I think that's where our relationship started to deteriorate. Too much time spent sacrificing the structure of our brains instead of talking to each other about our feelings. We never cared much for feelings. I tried resting my head on his shoulder one time and he shrugged me off. He was a great friend in a way, he was furious when a group of boys taxed me in the bathroom and threatened to smash all of their teeth inside the foyer. He taught me how to see the bad in the world and defend myself from it; ironically, I couldn't see that the worst threat to me was Fred himself. Still, he taught me to be cautious. We were companions once, but he probably learned nothing from me.

I met my current best friend in University. I read a poem about wanting to drive a van through the EA building and that night he dm'd me on Instagram and asked me if I wanted to write a poetry book. I had just previously been dropped by all of my closest friends, including Fred, and I was wary of people. Fred instilled a fear in me, he convinced me that everyone wore a mask. Receiving a compliment was always met with my discouragement, it always felt like a mockery, as if the other person was lying to me. Jake invited me out to his house in Priddis, and spending my whole life in the suburb, I was surprised by the countryside. We sat in his spacious basement, fingers clacking against macbook pro keyboards. Deers lurked in the trees peering at us from the thick layer of glass that embraced the pungent sun.

"What do you like to read?"

"I dunno," I responded. "Pretty much anything, I'm not good at branching out though."

Jake showed me his manga collection, encouraging me to read something other than shonen. He showed me *I Am A Hero*, the cover bearing the likeness of what has to be the main character standing on a pencil drawn, colorless bridge weaving a shotgun over his head.

"I like Cormac McCarthy," I told him. He proceeded to get me Blood Meridian for my birthday.

We go to concerts together and he introduces me to strange local indie bands that I otherwise wouldn't have heard of. On the way to Shelf Life getting off at 7th Street West Station, the dilapidated crosswalks of downtown and the jammed cars whir past our eardrums and fail to register in our frontal lobes as we discuss theory and people and literary movements and our aspirations of becoming authors.

Jake took me by surprise because to this day he has never made a joke at my expense. Whenever he compliments my writing I still flinch, expecting a backhand shortly afterwards but the backhand never comes. I stand awkwardly in front of him, leaning on the closet door so the skeletons don't come tumbling out. While Fred taught me to expect the worst in people, Jake taught me to be realistic. There's good and bad in people, but judging someone by deeming them a good or bad person isn't exactly something I can manage. I'm not God, then again, God is more like us than we like to believe. He can also be good and bad. He could've decided to forgive Eve, but he cursed her. His son screamed at him as his palms ached in agony and God let him die. Jake taught me that God is just like us. He too makes bad decisions. Be realistic. Don't have expectations for anyone but yourself.

    I met my girlfriend shortly afterwards in September, 2023. It was a Wednesday, I know because we met at Write Club, and her dark hair was long at the time contrasted by the green glint of her eyes. I won't go into detail, because I always get embarrassed, but she read a really good poem about love and in my mind we made eye contact a handful of times and she always likes to bring up how I melted into my seat. To this day she won't stop talking about it, but I don't mind. It's the kind of thing you sign up for when you get into a relationship.

    I came over for the first time on Thanksgiving. We weren't dating yet, and it was my first time meeting her family. We met at the train station and walked to her house and talked about school and programs and bullshit GNEDs and the south side of the city where I grew up versus the north side of the city and how I've never been in this part of Calgary before. It's older, but nicer in a way. The sidewalks are cracked in nostalgic fissures and the trees are large, challenging the authority of the sky and raining pinecones over non-artificial grass. The houses are wider instead of taller like they are in the deep south and the yards are massive adorned with complimentary firepits; so distinctly suburban.

We walked into her house and before going up the stairs she told me to make sure I shake her grandmother's hand. There she was, a small blond lady sitting meekly in a comfy reclining chair on a heap of blankets right next to the window facing the driveway. I walked over, my legs shaking, and I tried to steady myself as I reached out with a sweaty palm. She simply looked at me, a confused smile on her face. When I looked down, I discovered that Christina's grandmother lost her hands in World War II. I didn't leave after that, so things worked out pretty good.

I've never been good at expressing myself verbally. Fred taught me to swallow hatred and resentment, he taught me how to stomach the shit life feeds me. I let the rough lump of discomfort as I swallow become blades in my stomach that carve away at my insides until the anger dissipates. There's a lot I inherited from Fred. It's parents that raise us but it's friends that teach us to be social. Christina has taught me that I'm a good listener but I'm not a good communicator. I failed my driver's test the other day. The examiner sat next to me, casually explaining my fuck ups.

"Uncontrolled intersections, they're an automatic fail. You're supposed to slow down before reaching one."

"There's no stop or yield sign though," I said. "I have the right of way."

"Sure, but you have to look at the bigger picture. The driver on your right also thinks they have the right of way."

"There weren't any drivers coming."

"Still, you have to slow down. For next time, just imagine a stop or a yield sign."

"It shouldn't be my job to magically summon stop or yield signs. Uncontrolled intersections just go to show that our government is lazy."

"You think it's that easy to place signs on every road in the city?" He smirked, marking away on my fail sheet with a flicking wrist.

"Sure," I responded. "It was easy to colonize everything else a couple hundred years ago, yet you guys can't place down a couple of signs?"

The examiner sighed. He turned off his iPad and his hand moved towards the door handle. "Felix, I'm really sorry things didn't work out today."

"Sure you are, because you're getting paid a hundred and eighty-five dollars to fail me on a test-"

"Have a good day, Felix."

"-over a fucking technicality."

The car door slammed shut and I was left alone in my sister's corolla. My fingers curled into fists and for a moment I just sat. My mouth was wide open, air traveling freely from the stuffy atmosphere onto the road of my tongue and scraping my dangling uvula. I stared out grimly into the parking lot. I squeezed and unfurled my fingers and my vision turned red and I slammed my fist down on the car horn and shouted a muffled profanity before getting out of the white car and slamming the door.

I can recall it now, my fingers creating place markers on my keyboard. But I couldn't explain it to her.

"Tell me," she encouraged. "How do you feel?"

I looked at her and there was a quiver in her chin and a severity on her expression and I leaned in all at once and my head collapsed onto her shoulder. I didn't know what to say, I couldn't find the words with the emotions plaguing my mind, and I simplified it the best I could.

"I'm so fucking angry."

I never liked crying. Then again, nobody does. I cried a lot as a kid, way too much. Fred was annoyed by my sensitivity. I was taught to swallow my anger, and here she is, asking me to express it. I don't know how to explain it, but as embarrassed as I am, somehow, some way, I also feel better. The knot goes loose in my chest as I slump against her shoulder, and a shallow sob escapes the orifice of my skull. Christina taught me compassion. I think compassion is part of companionship. Compassion isn't always nice. It's asking someone to display the worst side of themselves and still choosing to love them for it. I'm trying to be better at expressing my emotions. I'm not turning down my mother every time she asks me how my day was. I'm trying to be honest. I'm not always the best at it.

look back
by Rachel Fitzgibbon

And if I can't take you home then we'll just stay here
Build a house in the mud
In the blood and filth and sinew
With ticks in the walls and fleas in the carpet
Spindly trees spilling shadows on our doorstep
Bears as our neighbours
The wolves as our dogs
Water damaged ceiling sagging over the wall
Rot stains framed as paintings
Where the water is always tinged brown
And the scent of sulphur never dissipates
Where everything is miserable except us
In this place of the unloved
I will love you enough to make it a home

And if I can't take you home then we'll just stay here
Until the world forgets our names
And we don't remember theirs
Where we have no one but each other
And need nothing more
No great myth will come of our story
No hymns written in our honour

look back
by Rachel Fitzgibbon

They will think I failed to save you
Then they will think of us no longer
And We will still be here
In this place where forgotten things live
Until we too are forgotten by all
And only we remember

And if I can't take you home then we'll just stay here
Home is not home without you
Empty arms weigh heavily on my heart
Too much to bear
I don't care where we are
If you cannot leave then I will not go
I won't leave you behind
If it kills me
You need me as much as I need you
And I'll damn the world to stay together

And though you want to leave
I know you can't go
So we'll stay in this place
And make it into our home.

The Gemini
(An Homage to Old Gemini by Radical Face)
by Bailey J. Wilson

When Jane had moved into the little cottage out in the country, she hadn't anticipated what it would bring her. The first few days had been lovely. After a drive to the shops to stock up on groceries, her days and nights were spent solely at the small cottage. Mornings were spent in the front garden, planting vegetables and herbs, letting the rich soil find a home under her nails. Her afternoons would be dedicated to housework: cooking, cleaning, and repairing the old furniture that had come with the house. In the evenings she would spend hours in front of the bay window reading, always with a steaming cup of Earl Grey in hand. It was perhaps a dull routine to some, but she loved the simplicity of it. She loved looking out into the garden and seeing it filled with fireflies at night, or watching the sunrise with her breakfast of toast, eggs, and coffee. It was a big difference from the life she had lived in her London flat, but Jane thought this was exactly what she needed after everything that had happened.

Her simple routine was interrupted one morning just as she had nearly finished planting for the day. Her trowel dug into the earth and instead of meeting the feeling of soft soil, it sank slightly before hitting something very solid. Jane lifted the trowel and dug down again but met the same resistance. She scooped up the dirt that she could and uncovered a metal container, roughly the size of a shoe box. Jane lifted it out and brushed the dirt off the top. The hinges were rusted, but the rest of the box seemed to be in fairly good condition, comparatively at least. There was a latch on the front but no lock holding it closed. Jane opened it carefully, concerned that the contents of the container may be something she didn't want to see. Whatever she had been expecting, it hadn't been the leather-bound journal that was sitting snugly inside.

The cover looked worn and the pages were tinged yellow, but it was in otherwise pristine condition. Despite the curiosity gnawing at her, Jane set the box to the side and finished planting the parsley. She returned her gloves and gardening tools to the shed and picked up the container to bring it inside the cottage. Forgoing her usual routine, she placed it on the side table by the bay window and carefully pulled out the journal, afraid it would somehow crumble in her hands. Thankfully, it was sturdier than it looked and she opened it to the first page.

THE JOURNAL OF EDWIN FRANCIS THOMSON

The loopy handwriting looked like something out of a period piece, and Jane found herself touching it reverently. The paper was soft with age and she feared just turning a page would tear one. Her eagerness to learn more about the mysterious author outweighed her concerns as she continued.

The Gemini
(An Homage to Old Gemini by Radical Face)
by Bailey J. Wilson

March 23rd, 1913

I am writing this because I am uncertain of how much time I have left on this earth. Though, I suppose, no one truly knows how much longer they will be among the living. I know I should find my death to be a much more terrifying concept, but I can't say that I am feeling much in the way of fear. Mother has moved us out of the city, I believe she hopes that the fresh air of the countryside will heal what the doctors could not. I hold no such illusions. This is by far the most painful part of this illness, being forced to watch my family watch me die. I worry for Jaime most of all. I truly could not imagine living without him by my side. From the moment we were born, we have been together, I do not envy him being the one to live. He is such a kind-hearted boy, I hate the thought of him facing the world without me. I worry that his kindness will be dimmed as he grows into adulthood.

As she finished reading the first entry, Jane felt a knot in her stomach. Perhaps she had been hoping for adventure and whimsy, or a fantastical love story; not the journal of a dying boy. Reading on, Jane found herself in awe of Edwin's wisdom. He mentioned several times that he had not reached adulthood, and never would, and Jane mourned the man he could have become.

She found herself struck with a need to immortalize his writing. Jane moved into her makeshift office and began typing out each entry in the old journal. She didn't know what she would do with

The Gemini
(An Homage to Old Gemini by Radical Face)
by Bailey J. Wilson

it, but something in her knew it was important for young Edwin's words to live on.

June 16th, 1913
   Our birthday has come and gone. Mother cooked us a wonderful dinner and each a small cake. I wish I had been able to enjoy it, but my appetite has been very poor as of late. We tried to celebrate, but I could see the sadness in Jaime and Mother's eyes. I look in the mirror and do not see myself, looking at Jaime is the only time I see myself now. I dread to see the flickers of this gaunt, pale boy who is in my reflection. I dread that this is who Jaime sees every day. Does he see me? Or does he see a glimpse of what he could have been in a different world? I have been thinking often about the cruelty of God. To have us born as a pair, but force one of us to spend the rest of his life alone. Where is the supposed love of God in that? Maybe it is the same cruelty that has me wishing for Jaime to live a long life without me. Regardless of it all, I know one thing for certain, Jaime helps me feel better about this end. It is selfish of me, but I know I will live on in him. I only wish he did not have to do so as one-half of a whole.

Edwin's birthday entry stuck with Jane long after she read it. His complex relationship with his own reflection and seeing his twin brother was something she couldn't shake. She felt his muted frustration and sadness in each loopy letter. As she continued reading

The Gemini
(An Homage to Old Gemini by Radical Face)
by Bailey J. Wilson

the words of a dying boy, she couldn't help but wonder what had happened to Jaime. How long had he lived? What had his life been like after losing Edwin? Did he have kids? Was there someone alive who would know about Edwin? Someone who would want to read this journal? Jane needed to learn everything she could. She knew how precious words from family were and she wanted to return these ones to the Thomsons.

A bittersweet sadness swelled within her as she flipped to the last page. This was the final piece of Edwin's writing; his last words to a world that he barely got to live in. The penmanship was noticeably sloppier, and the final line almost seemed to cut off abruptly. The effort it must have taken him to write this left Jane in awe. She took a deep breath and read Edwin Thomson's final entry.

August 27th, 1913

Jaime called me wise beyond my years, but my wisdom has only come from this situation I was forced into. Oncoming death brings much into perspective I suppose. I am so tired now. Writing these few sentences has taken so much. My last days have arrived, I know it. I have asked Mother to bury a box with this journal in the garden. I told her to give it to Jaime on our 18th birthday. He will have had time to grieve by then. To Jaime, my dearest brother, please live your best life. That is all I ask. There is more to be said but I am too weak to write anymore, I'm sorry. I am with you always, Jaime. Goodbye.

The Gemini
(An Homage to Old Gemini by Radical Face)
by Bailey J. Wilson

Jane sat back in her chair as tears rolled down her cheeks. Despite never knowing him, she felt as though she had also lost Edwin. Jane's desire to return the journal to the Thomson family had solidified. She wanted to fulfill Edwin's final wish to the best of her ability.

Thus, Jane dedicated herself to research and digging through archives and family trees. After a few months, she found the destination she had been searching for. She was endlessly thankful for having Edwin's whole name as it made the entire process easier. It had taken some work, and a lot of convincing the secretary in charge of the historical records, but it was all worth it as soon as she saw 'Edwin Francis Thomson' in a family tree connected to 'James Peter Thomson.' James, or Jaime as she had come to know him, had lived the long life his brother had hoped for him, dying in 1970 at the age of 71. He had married in 1924 and his wife had given birth to their first child, a boy named Edwin, in 1926. Their second child was born in 1928, a baby girl named Margaret. Although James, his wife, and their first son Edwin had passed on, Margaret was still alive. Margaret was also, to Jane's delight, living in an elderly care home only an hour's drive from the cottage. Now, Jane stood in front of Brynfield Care Home with a bag holding the journal at her side.

The young woman at the front desk had been kind and smiled politely as she led Jane to a table and told her she would go and get Margaret. Jane's leg bounced with nerves that only intensified as the nurse came towards the table with an elderly woman in a wheelchair.

The Gemini
(An Homage to Old Gemini by Radical Face)
by Bailey J. Wilson

"Margaret, this is Jane Williams. She wants to talk to you about your father," the nurse explained as Margaret waved her hand dismissively.

"You told me that already, my memory isn't that bad yet. The day you have to repeat something you told me less than 5 minutes ago is the day I step into oncoming traffic." Jane snorted at the dark joke as the nurse flushed slightly. She stepped away from the table leaving Margaret and Jane alone.

"Um,"

Jane felt unsure now that the moment was here. Would Margaret even care about a journal from an Uncle who had died long before she was ever born? The elderly woman raised an eyebrow in prompting and Jane cleared her throat.

"I recently moved into a cottage about an hour from here, and I found a box when I was digging in the garden. There was a journal in the box that I believe belonged to your father's brother." Jane lifted the box out of her bag and pulled out the journal, placing it on the table in between them.

Margaret's eyes were wide as she flipped open the first page with shaking hands. Her fingers touched Edwin's written name with the same reverence that Jane herself had felt upon first seeing it.

"I know he died long before you were born but-"

"Uncle Edwin," Margeret interrupted with an awed whisper. "Dad talked about him all the time. Told Ed and me stories about his twin brother and..." Her other hand came up and covered her mouth. A range of emotions crossed her face as she flipped through the pages.

The Gemini
(An Homage to Old Gemini by Radical Face)
by Bailey J. Wilson

"I read the entire journal, and I hope you don't mind, but I also typed out each entry. I just wanted to preserve his writings, but I felt that the journal itself should go to his family." Jane fidgeted with her fingers on the table, holding her breath as she hoped Margaret wouldn't be angry about the invasion into her family history.

"Oh, no dear I- Dad always told us how smart Uncle Edwin was and how he wished he had been able to share that genius with the world. Dad always said he was wise beyond his years..." Margaret's eyes shone with tears and Jane felt her own welling up.

"His words were deeply moving. I..." Jane looked down at the table, watching her thumbs spinning around each other. "I recently lost my twin sister to cancer. I always wondered what she had been thinking in those last months and this... I feel like I've gotten a glimpse into what her final months must have been like and I-" Margaret's hand came to rest on top of Jane's and she looked up, meeting the old woman's eyes. "I'm very grateful to him," Jane finished, letting out a deep breath. It felt like she had been holding that breath since she'd gotten the call that Emily was dead.

"Would you tell me about her? Your sister?" Margaret asked, squeezing Jane's hand with a reassuring smile.

"I would love to."

Ellie
by Sylvia Belcher

You'd be surprised how much dust settles when something is left too long. I don't know how long it's been now, only that the dust is thick enough that I look through a hazy veil upon the shop below me. I can't blink dust away like people can. My blonde curls are surely grey with it now. I mark the days only by the ding of the bell as The Old Man enters with the muted sunlight, and the ding of it as he leaves with the hazy orange. If porcelain could be stiff I would be. If I could stretch out my legs and arms and let out a long sigh of relief I would. Ellie would have stretched them out, if she knew I was here. Ellie would make sure I got to sit on the grass next to her during a picnic on a sunny day. If I fell off the bed she would kiss me to make sure I knew she loved me, and that she was sorry I slipped. And at the end of the day, she wouldn't leave with a ding. She would tuck me warm into the crook of her arm, and I'd feel her soft breath whoosh through my curls. Ellie would brush off every bit of dust – Ellie would never let dust land or settle to begin with. But Ellie's not here. And where does that leave me? That leaves me with nothing of the purpose I was built with. I remember everything. That's the curse of a strangely immortal, but unalive life. Your mind never changes, never fades if you don't have a brain. Everything that happens stays. You stay. Exactly the same, day in and day out. But nothing else does. Everything changes, everything fades. Dies. But not you. You just remember. And collect some dust.

Ellie
by Sylvia Belcher

And pray you could close your eyes and sleep. I remember the green and red box I was wrapped up in under the tree. I remember the giddiness that bubbled in my chest as I waited, week in and week out for the lid to be lifted. I'd lay in that box and just listen—I could hear her voice, the way she was so quick to giggle. She sang, my Ellie. All the time. If she wasn't singing, she was humming. I remember the humming got so close one day, so close I felt the box vibrate against my porcelain. I just knew her face was right there by my box—I just knew she was as excited to meet me as I was her—I just knew she was trying to gauge what I was based on shape alone. She was strictly told not to shake anything, as it may break. If I could giggle I would have, with her there that close. I waited and waited, and tided myself over with her footsteps and melodious voice. And then it finally happened. There was a rush of scurrying footsteps down the stairs, and gleeful little squeals.

"Alright girls, let's do this in an orderly fashion!" A jovial voice boomed. And then—light! And oh. There she was. Ellie. My Ellie. With her freckles and bright eyes, her auburn curls falling all around her face and shoulders. She lit up when her gaze met mine, and when she smiled—oh that gap-toothed smile. She pulled me into her warm, soft chest. And I was home. From that day on I fulfilled my purpose day in and day out.

She'd go to school every day of course, and she'd give me a kiss on the face, say "I love you forever." And rush out the door. I'd wait all day, and wish desperately I could swing my legs to let off some of the enthusiasm. I'd watch the clock hands tick, and finally when the

Ellie
by Sylvia Belcher

big hand reached down, and the small hand reached to the right, the door would click open and oh, how my heart would soar. She'd burst in and swing me around, and out into the world we'd go. She'd place me firmly into the basket of her bicycle, tearing down the street to meet Bobby and Em. The wind would frisk through my locks, relentlessly streaming across my face and always open eyes. The exhilaration was the most I've ever known. On one occasion, on the way to the treehouse, Ellie hit a bump and I went soaring into the sky—it was fun for a moment, before I remembered that I am not flesh and a bandage probably wouldn't do much in the way of help.

"No!" Ellie screeched as the ground tumbled, trading places again and again with the sky. It rushed up to meet me, and I felt my arm crack. I looked over to see it lying beside me. What a bother I remember thinking, because of course it didn't hurt. What did hurt was hearing the howls that emerged from Ellie as she ran towards me, tripping and sliding, hands splayed out towards me. She pushed off the ground and picked me up, a tear falling and landing on my porcelain, right beneath my eye, and trailing off my face.

"I'm so sorry" she sobbed, and I wished with everything I was I could tell her I didn't hurt. I tried to tell her with my eyes.

That night Ellie's mother helped to glue my arm back on. "Alright Dr. Ellie, let's put on our doctor's coats!" Ellie's Mom said.

Ellie laughed, and they both pulled on invisible coats. "Next, let's listen for her heartbeat!" Ellie leaned in close, pretending to listen. I wished I could beat for her. "Yep! All good!"

Ellie
by Sylvia Belcher

"Excellent, excellent! Well, it seems as if our patient just needs a little glue and she will be back on track!" I watched as Ellie's Mom gently brushed glue onto the jagged end of my detached arm, and pushed it back into place. Ellie's eyes misted up, and then softened. "Just be gentle with her for a while, alright? She might need some healing time." All the healing time I needed was seeing Ellie's gap-toothed smile return.

The thing about little girls is, they don't stay little girls. It was easy to forget that when summer days stretched out long and many ahead of me. When I got to sit next to her in the treehouse, popsicle melt dried on my face after she tried to share with me. One day she started to stare in the mirror a little longer at her face. She had red freckles now on top of her usual ones. She cried when they appeared, and I couldn't understand why. I always thought her freckles were so beautiful. She cried a lot those days. And laughed a lot still. She seemed so happy one moment, and so so sad the next. I didn't get to go outside much anymore, but I still got to sleep with her every night, and when she was sad, I got to comfort her in her arms. On lucky days, when nobody was looking, she would still sneak me into the garden to have breakfast next to her. I loved those lucky days. The sun felt good on my face.

Time pressed on, and suddenly there was Toby. Toby came over when Mom and Dad were at work. Ellie would rush into the room, frenzied, and I'd try to make my ever-still smile wider for her.

Ellie
by Sylvia Belcher

She'd rush towards me, and my heart would light up, hoping I might just once more be whisked away for an adventure to the treehouse. But her hand wrapped around me just to turn me away, towards the wall, so I couldn't see the room anymore. She made noises–happy ones, I think, and so I was happy. If Toby made Ellie happy, then I liked Toby.

Toby stopped coming around. Ellie didn't make happy sounds anymore. Or happy faces. She stayed in bed a long, long time. If my heart was real, it would have broken alongside hers. I stood on that shelf a long while. She didn't get up. I wished so hard I could call out to her, or just walk over and pat her back until she stopped shaking. I'd never been more aware of how still I was.

At some point Ellie's Mom came in. I tried with everything I was to look at her imploringly, hoping she might comfort Ellie the way I might have if I could. She sat on Ellie's bed a long time, with her hand drawing circles on the back of her pyjamas. Ellie's sobs kept up. Ellie's Mom had this look in her eyes I'd never seen before. She looked–lost. I tried to catch her gaze. Eventually, she did look up, and I felt as if my heart might have skipped a beat. She walked over to me, picked me up, and just held me tight to her chest for a long while. I felt her chest quake a little, before she took a deep, steadying breath and walked me towards Ellie. "Here, El. Someone wants to say hi to you." Ellie's Mom tucked me into Ellie's arm, which was wet with tears, but warm. Ellie pulled me in close, breathing in the smell of my hair, and finally

Ellie
by Sylvia Belcher

stopped crying. I lay in her arms until her breath became even and measured, and she was asleep. My Ellie.

After a few years of sitting on Ellie's shelf, she came home one day squealing. She dashed into my room, scooped me up and spun me around. "I'm getting married! I'm getting married!"

We moved into a new home that fall. I liked my new spot, up on a shelf. I could tell Edward–her Husband, felt a little strange about having me there, but he didn't say anything, which made me happy. My days there were quiet, peaceful. Sometimes I missed Ellie's Mom. The best I got those days was hearing her voice in the kitchen when she came to visit—she sounded cheery, what more could I ask for?

And then one day, after sitting there for what felt like a long time, Ellie came rushing in, yanked me off my shelf, spun me around, and sang "I'm having a baby, I'm having a baby!"

Benjamin was...loud. But oh he was round. Rosy and rolly, with exactly zero teeth.

I loved him. From up on my shelf I loved him with my whole heart. One day, Ellie held Ben in her arms and rocked back and forth in the newly added rocking chair, singing in that voice of hers–still as sweet as the first day I heard it. While she rocked him, she looked up at me. She stood, Ben cradled in one arm, and walked up to my shelf. She lifted me down, cradling me in her other arm and sat back down

Ellie
by Sylvia Belcher

in the chair. "Benny, this is a very dear friend of mine. She's taken care of me all my life." I looked into his big, watery blue eyes. There was so much life, so much wonder in those eyes. I wished I had tear ducts.

I watched the montage of his life from the shelf, in bits. I mostly listened, as he came into his parents' room less and less as he got older. I saw him lots as a baby, being lifted from his crib and rocked. I watched Ellie's face as the circles around her eyes got darker and darker. I would have taken a turn rocking him if my body weren't so small and solid. I watched him through the toddler stages, terrorizing anything he could get his little hands on. I noticed Ellie's exasperation, but the affection in her eyes outweighed it every time. I watched him become a teenager. He yelled a lot. I was there when Ellie got the phone call, when her panicked voice filled the room as she rushed from the house, the door slamming behind her. The house was empty for a few days after that. I felt ill with worry. Where was my Ellie? When she came home, she was pushing a wheelchair, Ben sitting in it, slumped over in devastation. He slept in a foldout bed in Ellie's room for a long time after that.

Eventually Ben left. I heard Ellie's voice from the front door "You're going to do so well Benny. You show them who Benjamin Blake is." The minute the door clicked, Ellie dissolved into sobs I hadn't heard in a long time. She came into the room, pulled me down, lay in her bed and curled her body around me. She sobbed into me for what must have been hours until she fell asleep. I realized then that I

Ellie
by Sylvia Belcher

couldn't remember the last time I had slept in her bed with her. Couldn't recall the last time she put me on the shelf one night and never took me to comfort her again. I felt myself relax into her, as much as porcelain can, and savoured the feeling of her breath once again against me.

There were many sleepy days after that. I watched the sun rise and set day after day from my shelf. I was never sad though, knowing each night I'd get to watch Ellie climb into bed, and roll over to lay on Edward's chest. I noticed as it became harder for her to lift her leg up onto the bed. Silver began to streak through her auburn curls. I still thought she was pretty as ever.

There were grandkids. They were busy. Of all four tumbling, rolling, screeching children, one stuck out to me. She looked ever so much like Ellie. One day, I was listening to the happy twittering child sounds, when the door creaked open, and she walked in. Amanda. She must have been about six. She stood there, staring up at me, bright eyes and freckles.

"Hi dolly." She said, "You must be so lonely up there all on your own." The door creaked open again. She jumped. "Oh! I was just looking Grandma, I promise!"

"That's okay sweetie," Ellie said "Let me take her down for you." Ellie lifted me and placed me in Amanda's arms. Her dimples emerged with her smile.

"Oh, she's lovely."

Ellie
by Sylvia Belcher

"Yes she is. She's an old friend of mine. One day, when I'm gone, I want her to be yours." Amanda's head turned quickly to look Ellie in the eye.

"Really?" It was then I realized....gone. One day Ellie would be gone.

After that day I savoured every moment of Ellie, every word, every laugh, every touch. Edward went first. He stopped coming home one day and suddenly it was me in Ellie's bed every night. She cried longer than she ever had before, and I looked at his picture on her nightstand sometimes, just trying to thank him with my eyes, for all the years he made my Ellie so happy. I tried not to be mad he wasn't around anymore. Humans can't stay the way we can.

We moved again, to a small room, with a window view of a rose garden. I liked the view. I liked the old ladies that came around to visit Ellie for tea. I realized one day she was an old lady too. She was slow now. Everything took her three times as long to do. But she never stopped doing. And she never stopped humming. I wished I could help her make her tea, and bring her a book when she was too stiff to want to roll over in bed and grab it herself. But I had realized at some point that all the wishing in the world wasn't going to change me, and that all I could do was watch her live, and commit my own life to loving her.

Ellie
by Sylvia Belcher

One sunny day, Ellie brought me out into the garden. She placed me in the basket of her walker the way she used to on her old bike, and we sat in the chair by the roses. It was the first time I'd felt the sun on my porcelain in a long time. Ellie's eyes were closed in bliss as I looked up at her weathered face from her arms. Her freckles were still spotted there between lines. She opened her eyes after a long while, looked me in the face and whispered "I love you forever." She held me tight to her chest and I listened to her heart thump, thump, thump. And not a single thump more.

I felt as if every piece of my porcelain was cracked after that. In the chaos of sorting out her possessions, I got tossed in the wrong box. And now I'm here. I have been, for a long, long time. I'm grey with dust the way Ellie was grey with age now. I wish I had a spirit, so maybe I could die and be with Ellie too. Edward is lucky, up there with her.

***

"Mommy, is that her?" After years of resignation, I finally mustered up the strength to try to look through the dust in my eyes. It was too thick to see now. Someone lifted me from the shelf. Someone lifted me from the shelf! A hand brushed against my eyes and oh! It couldn't be! Freckles. Amanda.
"Oh my goodness, it is her!" I could have cried at the sight of those curls, those dimples. She passed me down to a little girl below. If I thought Amanda looked like Ellie, it was nothing compared to this girl.

Ellie
by Sylvia Belcher

"Grandma wanted us to have her right?"

"That's right sweetie. She took care of Grandma all her life, and now she's yours to care for."

The girl held me tight to her chest, and whispered "I'll love you forever."

Darlene
by Sylvia Belcher

Tell me again about the birds
How the starlings signal first spring.
Hold out cracked blue eggs
And tell me who belonged to them.
Show me the way you crow out into the sky
So a black feathered phantom will sweep down
Trusting enough to feed.

You are home here among the trees and the creatures
I see you, elven and wise.
Upon turning into your drive
I watch you, sat upon a stump.
Tangles of plants twine around your calves
Accepting you as their own.
You belong so much to the wild world,
I can't imagine you caged and kept.

When you take me for a wander
Through your precious sanctuary of land
For me, you unearth every hidden thing.
Mushrooms bursting up from the ground
That bring forth plumes beneath your foot.

Darlene
by Sylvia Belcher

Tiny purple lamps of fairies
Grown in their own micro meadows.
Soft aspen skin that gifts chalky white powder
Spread upon faces to ward off scorching sun.

You seem solid as a wooden trunk,
Rooted.
Your skin wrinkles like bark,
Years of grooves written in.
You commune with God in the trees
Reached in ways church could not.

When we speak, we spar.
We throw wit like paper stars
Unfolding each one
To see their lines of creation.
I watch you twinkle
As I let forth my wildness.
Unabashed and honest.
I laugh without shame
And look challengers dead in the eye
Unflinching.

In the fields we watch hawks circle overhead.
You too have feathered wings
Marked by bands used to tie them.

Darlene
by Sylvia Belcher

You were too young
To stave off the hands that did.
I want to massage out the wounds,
Make your plumage lay smooth once more.
Despite its grooves, it shines.

In your eyes is a girl with a snake round her neck
Reigning terror over city folk
Defiantly steadfast
Refusing her skirts
Flashing animal teeth and shrieking for freedom.

But they twisted your small limbs
And crammed you in a box
Which might have been your coffin
If you'd lain.

But you scratched
Till at once
You clawed your way out
Shredding your cardboard prison.
Like a feline far from home
You at last made your escape
Back to the prairie
Guided by an inner compass begging your getaway.

Darlene
by Sylvia Belcher

When I hunt down my ambitions,
It is for you.
You and our long lineage of those told to sit down.

My wings beat relentlessly,
Sun break to set
Fuelled by thoughts of aprons and regrets
And generations of heavy fists.
I refuse to be silenced
No heavy-racked buck will ever make me small.

When I dream, it will be of you on your land
Digging in your feet and declaring
Making clear
You will not be dragged from your sanctuary,
Your home, your being.

When I hear the call of a morning bird
It's your voice hitting my ears.
When I press my hand into moss,
It is your embrace I receive.
When I breathe crisp air
You fill my lungs.

I was born of the forest nymphs,
You, the matriarch of the line.

Darlene
by Sylvia Belcher

Our souls composed of wind
Our hair of the ebbing grasses
Our blood the babble of winding creeks.
When you speak of the wilderness
You speak of ourselves.
So tell me again about the birds.

A Year Apart
by Myra Monday

We are back where we started
A year apart
Same place
New people
Still strangers
So much can change in a year
We met, we laughed, we smiled
We spent so much time together
We learned so much about each other
I learned how to love
I learned I loved you
We had grown so close
You were all I ever wanted
All I ever thought I needed
You helped me grow strong
Become more confident
More happy
When you left, I cried over you
The most I have over anyone
I was hurt
Was it all a lie?
Did you ever truly see me the way you described?

A Year Apart
by Myra Monday

The way I thought I was seen in your eyes
I missed you
I wanted so badly to know if you hurt too
If you missed me as much as I did you
How much I wanted to know why
Why you left
Why now?
Why me?
How much I wanted to ask
Get answers
Get closure
But that wouldn't be fair to you
Trying you keep you for just a little longer
Trying to piece together what went wrong
Taking out my grief and anger on you
I didn't want to hold you back anymore
I knew you had already moved on
And a wound can't heal
If the thing that caused it is still stuck inside the flesh
So life went on without you
I met new people
I tried new things
Relearning who I was without you
Appreciating the parts of me I still see you in
Parts that would not exist if you had never made a mark on my life
I had found new things to love:

A Year Apart
by Myra Monday

Sunsets, the moon, the stars
Being outside, feeling the wind, taking a breath
I learned to love life
I learned to love myself
And I still thought about you
Remembering our time spent together
Our connection, what we had, what we once were
Knowing it'll never be what it once was
Finding peace that it'll never be what it once was
Yet I still wondered how you were doing
What you were doing
And now I find you again
In the same place we first met
Having lived a lifetime in that single year
Having grown and changed into new people
Reminding myself that you are not the same person you once were
And neither am I
Meeting your familiar face
As a stranger once again
With the bittersweet knowledge that we can never truly restart
Yet happy I get to meet you again
That our paths still cross
And I get to meet the person who I had once loved

Even when you feel like a stranger.

Tracking in Eight Parts
by Brennan Kenneth Brown

∅.
Let me tell you. The things we carry are the things we let die. Memory static fuzzes between channels. Tracking, tracking, tracking. Tracking.

I.
Aluminum foil on rabbit ears clothes-hanger. Screen snow is dandruff for the television. Between Saturday morning cartoons and fuzz lived a hippo. Not behemoth wading through African rivers, but *The North American House Hippo*—no bigger than a mouse, gathering lint and dryer sheets for nesting in the bedroom closet. The PSA meant to teach us media literacy. We just, instead, yearned for impossible pets. I hunt for reuploads of these commercials on YouTube at 3 in the morning, the VHS tracking lines a comfort blanket. Over-the-top YTV bumpers, the PJ Fresh Phil era, the computer-animated talking robot head. The Concerned Children's Advertisers logo burning into my retinas as ghost image. Every memory of childhood is product placement, my joy branded™. Missing childhood means missing the commercials that interrupted our youth and escapism from pre-divorce arguments. Our nostalgia is hypercapitalist. What we remember is underwritten by corporations long defunct and dead. We are the last generation to remember the grief of the VHS tape eating

our favourite recordings. the staticky consolation of adjusting tracking on a second-hand cathode-ray television. Low-resolution glimpses of *Quién* era. Basic cable, local car dealership jingles outliving the salesman.

II.
Watch face glows ghost-blue at midnight. Numbers climb like fever. A few years ago I was diagnosed with paroxysmal supraventricular tachycardia. It is, more than anything, a totally benign diagnosis. My heart gallops in morse code. I check my EKG again. Again. Again. The graph spikes and valleys like a skyline I'm falling from. As a kid, I could dissolve into maladaptive daydreams, build universes between commercial breaks. My imagination corrodes with each pulse check. Five minutes pass. I tap the crown again. The body becomes a betrayal, each sensation a possible ending. My right arm tingles—heart attack or just anxiety? Both need rituals. Both need prayers. I document each premature atrial contraction. A scientist studying his own extinction. There's so much work left undone, so many stories still banking in my blood. There's still so much love poetry left to write. I want to live long enough to finish everything, to write it all down. But I also want to live for the selfish miracle of morning light through stained glass, for the way certain songs sound at 3AM, for the specific shade of purple the sky turns before snow. Somewhere between these watch-face confessions and childhood dreams lies the truth: I am afraid of dying before I've lived enough to justify all this borrowed time. The

EKG reads "normal sinus rhythm" but what's normal about watching your own heart try to escape its cage? Numbers climb. I check again.

III.
Dust motes dance in florescent light. Radiators tick like retiring timepieces. The Humanities department lounge on the third floor is my real home now. After being locked away for two years because of COVID. When Dr. Meinser finally had it reopened I spent days cleaning the innocuous minifridge and time-capsule microwave with mold-as-specimen. Arranging the octogonal tables just so, hanging tapestries celebrating nobody's birthday anymore. The shelves grown with liberated textbooks—no different than freedoms bought through LibGen and Z-Library and Anna's Archive. Piracy is praxis. Paper signs haphazardly printed out read "FREE BOOKS (REALLY)" because nobody believes in gifts anymore. Nothing walks away here. The fancy pens I left stay put. The good cardstock paper remains pristine. Spaces, certain spaces, resist the market. Rooms, certain rooms, remember how to be commons. The halls smell of burnt coffee and theory, of overeager highlights of passages in borrowed books. No tragedy here, except I'm leaving. I'm leaving the quiet revolution of shared resources, of knowledge freed from paywalls and profit margins. Sixty grand in debt and all I really know is this: the Milky Way room belongs to everyone. The logic of scarcity falls apart like wet newsprint.

IV.

She drives a silver Jeep older than most freshmen. She offers me a ride up north when I'm catsitting for an ex. I count kilometer marks like prayer beads. Pine air freshener, swaying. Dashboard Jesus nods in agreement. We're both mature students. Between classes I watch compilations of ancient television wondering if she grew up seeing the same thing. Cookie Crisp, Crossfire, Sock'em Boppers. *"More fun than a pillow fight!"* I have no employment history for the past five years except the writing of papers analyzing the Queer nature of Shakespeare, who I don't even believe was a real person (and my professors enrage when I bring up the topic). But her carpool playlist included Pink Pony Club and American Football, I think that's worth more than a pension plan.

V.

Phone screens burn human-blue at midnight. Thumbs hover, uncertain. My brother sometimes texts memes I don't understand. I want to tell him about Billy-Ray Belcourt or Joshua Whitehead, about sprung rhythm and the terrible beauty of God. I want to explain why I spend so much time in this brutalist building reading dead people's mail. Instead, I send him reaction emojis hoping some wisdom transfers through cultural osmosis. How do you be the kind of older brother who makes the path easier without smoothing away all the important rough edges? Every day I practice dying. Practice leaving him. My legacy needs to be more substantial than a good YouTube playlist and annotated poetry. My brother pours drinks at a Mexican bar, became an expert in tequila. The worms are rare, he says. I pretend that he mixes cocktails with the same precision I use to parse semicolons. He started coming to write club, then left a girl's heart cracked open. I tried to joke that he should enroll, to take over as president after I graduate. He just keeps wiping down the counter. A growing and gaping maw of distance. Slang ages like milk. He's twenty-two and knows more about real life. Nightly tips worth more than my poetry.

VI.
Matches scratch universe into being. Smoke curls in cursive. In the morning, I light the sage bundle. Cedar. Tobacco. Rosemary from the grocery store wearing a barcode. The alarms and detectors glare with a single red eye. The cat sniffs disapprovingly. Ceremony is doing something over and over until it becomes true. Peel an orange and it's a ritual. Drink water and it's a prayer. Walking the red road means paying attention. Everything is relatives. Even the student loan statements and being an asshole and drunken unsent texts. Spirit-walking between worlds. Be careful to not let the holy smoke choke out the profane lungs, or trigger colonial panic. Respect everything, waste nothing. I microwave leftover bannock at 2 in the morning. The ceremony is done right.

VII.
Mirror shows a stranger's face. I am everything I pretend to dismantle. I am performance, not practice. I have a collection of decolonization

Tracking in Eight Parts
by Brennan Kenneth Brown

in my Zotero while my Mamere's language dies in my mouth. I write essays about anti-Neoliberalism on a MacBook Pro. I speak land acknowledgements for institutional events while paying tuition funding colony, funding genocide. The smoke from store-bought sage reaches the fire alarm, not my ancestors. I am a softened, unrecognizable, theory-drunk bastard of their bloodline. I tell myself sharing PDFs is praxis while my brother works real jobs, lives in the real world. My nostalgia for children's commercials is deeper than my knowledge of my own culture's stories. The digital archives of capitalism hold more of my memories than the oral tradish. I perform authenticity for white professors mistaking my academic vocabulary for wisdom. The best thing I could do for decolonization is shut up and listen, but here I am, writing more words, taking up more space. The hippo was a lie, but so am I.

VIII.
My ancestors knew how to read pressed grass, interpret broken twigs, follow paths invisible. Tracking deer through morning, read stories in muddy riverbanks. Warm soot nearby. Tracking, tracking, tracking. Tracking. Sometimes I dream about my brother's future. In the dream, I've finally figured out how to be wise sans preaching, how to give advice without angering him, to protect the lungs without suffocating the smoke. I've learned how to share the important things, the real stuff about how to be a person in this world with hope and love and optimism despite everything. In the dream, I die peacefully, knowing I've done this one thing right. But I wake up still wondering.

Tracking in Eight Parts
by Brennan Kenneth Brown

Trying to translate between generations and worldviews. The sacred and mundane, the mundane and profane. But maybe you can believe in the spaces between commercials, in borrowed cars and borrowed books, in smoke prayers and shared stories. Maybe that's enough. Maybe all we can do is leave behind free textbooks and unlocked rooms, small acts of resistance against the machinery of profit. Die gently knowing we tried to make the path softer for those who follow, even as the path itself disappears into wilderness.

Art by Kenneth Gordon

"Dear Nina"
by Mark (Marcus) Vertodazo

When you look in a mirror
do you see petal shards
of sliced spring sun flowers
residing across the table margins
of yr soft smile?
Do you see the endless shades
of eclipsing sunlight
highlight how yr tresses of hair,
coated individually in scintillated honey,
kips up into straight house shue steps,
capoeira *rasteiras* & buttery twists?
Do you see how yr hopes for humanity,
sprouts from each column of my rib-cage
when I stand solemnly amongst yr optimistic presence?
Beside your still shadow
my emotions are amplified,
my empathy is augmented a hundred-fold;
I swear to God
your heartbeat is a boon to all beings,
a resounding call to be bold and benevolent & how it should be a
mandatory necessity for all working-class civilians of society
to be comfortable in yr own skin.
Do you know how now

"Dear Nina"
by Mark (Marcus) Vertodazo

my hope has me in a choke hold,
wrenching / evoking / reminding me
that I should breathe
& let sunlight seep / summon / express
itself straight into the sprouting blood vessels of my chafed skin?
& so beneath this scattering raincloud
of my self-contained consciousness;
I come to terms that my eczema scarred skin will always be scratched,
will always be sore with several self-inciting crop circles scathed
upon, stockpiling sandpiles of scales that scale up the walls of my
bedroom & sleep beside the spiked popcorn.
Even if it may shatter,
even if it may weep and shed,
it is still skin that has lived
and that is the lesson.

"Dear Shan"
by Mark (Marcus) Vertodazo

Yr aura reminds me always of warmth;
the sunrise radiance that comes with gentle reminders
to slow down whilst the window
reflects the reams of sunlight to soak into my skin.
Yr laugh reminds me of the uninterrupted wind
that indiscriminately dances in endless windmills
between the sprouting mangosteen leaf stems,
the clean smell of pho broth, & weighted chopsticks
tall as skyscraper shadows.
Yr energy reminds me of the monday raze
of morning rush trac; coarse, chaotic & impromptu,
but you still manage to give me goosebumps in the best way
possible.
Yr breath reminds me that sometimes i need to allow my body
to be blown away alongside these bellows of clouds,
to become dense in inertia, to always be autonomously suspended in
a sense of serene while fully ashed
in a golden crisp humble I caught the knick of time.
you are the empty space
in self-help colouring books,
which means to say:
you are the drowning white that thins out the bolded lines

"Dear Shan"
by Mark (Marcus) Vertodazo

i've drawn recklessly around my limbs
in moments of struggle and the taunting need of self-assurance; my
self diagnosed autopsy. but you remind me that scribbling is therapy
in itself, so i attempt to make my scribbles resemble strawberry
bushes thriving and ripening, and take those
around you, whilst you're in yr silly splendor
my condense stands oh so tall, accentuated,
my spine extended fully and shoulders cranked back,
beside you. i see yr presence and the looming stench of cigarettes and
cannabis strains around you a complete blessing, as you remind me
to hold my head high, and raise my palms to the gleaming sun, to
treat myself like a fresh potted sunflower plant and reach for more,
as if i truly deserved it all in the first place.

"Limerence — A Triptych Series"
by Mark (Marcus) Vertodazo

One.
CrossIron Mall.
Curtain bangs, covered in crepe & cotton
covering a canvas-wide forehead,
lining each connecting coastline
on the edge of her oceanic eyes.
Copper coated in roasted chestnuts
& charred chocolate,
an atoll of russet coral reefs,
cushions of cremated lavender,
tobacco & kush
concealed within
a cigarette / cuban cigar papers / cassava leaves,
crimped / crumpled / compacted
no,
no,
no, correction:
caressed with stiletto length nails.
Car windows coddled in raincloud tears,
counting how many clumped up batches
of raindrops have congregated upon this transparent colosseum,
watching this first viewing of a connection freshly flourishing.

"Limerence — A Triptych Series"
by Mark (Marcus) Vertodazo

Coveting alongside the strong scent
of burnt Circle-K corner store corridors
of plastic / disintegrated papers / chamomile pistils.
A hot-boxed bouquet
of camellas & freshly snatched lavenders
recklessly plucked from a government buildings owerbed whilst
cruising on a cracked cruiser board,
crazily cutting lines in between citizens
alike the coarse curves of a turquoise crystal.

Two.
Me, myself & I;
melting into a multitude
of amaranth / magenta / watermelon dyed marigolds, immersed,
marinated, submerged into headlight mirrors & De La Soul in
stereo.
Amber / mango / vermillion,
chromas of a matte orange sunset I chased:
130 on Deerfoot Trail to be with you again.
Stratus / cumulus / cirrus clouds masking templates into the
atmosphere, the thermosphere, the backspace of my mind who
chooses to continuously
ruminate / ponder / muse ;
on my modern day memories
of mutual laughter & slight mania.

"Limerence — A Triptych Series"
by Mark (Marcus) Vertodazo

Three.
Do you know
how many lifetimes
I would trade in to see your smile
its truest form; to witness a shard
or a single woodstripped sliver of a smirk
seep past your menacing side-eye?
To see cedar saplings & carnation stems
seep out your scarred / mangled / gnarled gums from the copious
amounts of chain smoking you indulge in?
To have you hold banquets on my lower back, adorned with frilly
flower beds of carnations
& stulls of baby's breath
expel out each column of my spine
in exchange for my soul
who'd write endless reams of poetry
until the ink of my pen
paints a landscape for me to sleep in.
If I could;
I would spend semesters surveying the way
shadows sculpt around certain curves of yr cheeks,
I would remember every freckled crater
& every little mole that blisters in-between,
I would remember every acne scar
that stands on the surface of yr skin
& still build the foundation

"Limerence — A Triptych Series"
by Mark (Marcus) Vertodazo

of my home on top of that.
I often think about what to put
on the last page of my will
and I think I nearly figured it out.
Let them know that every bit of my life insurance was entrusted in yr
presence, let them know I invested my life savings into yr laughter,
let them know that I lived my life loudly and allowed my love to
become a tumultuous entity beyond this physical body.
Let them know that if you ever need me;
play the song "pasilyo" in front of my resting place
& I will punch through the ground at an instant,
gripping on the realization that regardless
of the countless piles of poetry I write,
my favourite prayer will always be you.

Fog of the Lost
by Levi Hunstad-Neighbour

I stare into the swirling fog, unable to see further than ten steps. I have no sense of direction and no way to get home, I am lost. Aimlessly wandering with no end in sight I start to think, *what is my destination? Why do I have to go anywhere? Nobody cares if I just stay in this fog.* I try to hold in my fear as the fog begins to thicken. This is the end. I stop, taking a moment to catch my breath. I think about all the things I wanted to do with my life – go on an adventure, fall in love, become part of something bigger, be heartbroken, learn to take care of myself, all the things I've ever heard about.

I pick a direction and continue to walk; the cold, hard ground sends shockwaves up my tired legs. I try to think of my time before the fog, but nothing comes to mind. The dead trees and grass that blot in and out of existence are the only relief I have from the constantly shifting fog. With no visible reference points beyond the fog's walls, I decide to count my journey in steps. Hopefully, the counting will help keep me sane while I look for a way out.

Time passes and I feel like I have made no progress. Every tree I pass looks like the one before it. The air begins to get colder and my vision becomes obscured, causing each breath to sting as the fog's vapor enters my lungs. I can only see a few feet in any direction and decide to stop and take a break, sitting down to rest my tired legs. *Should I keep walking this way, or should I try a different direction?* I let this question sit with me for a while. The fog starts to recede and I stand up and continue in the same direction.

I walk for what feels like days, taking small breaks to recover my strength. My thoughts wander and new ideas emerge with every few steps I take. *I wonder if there is anyone else out here? How long have I been alone? What if I never get out? Should I just die here?* The sound of my feet is the only thing breaking the complete silence, but even my walking fades into nothing as the silence turns to loneliness, the loneliness to fear, the fear to despair, and then the despair turns to hope, hope as something new catches my eye.

On my right, the fog seems to change from its usual gray, and there seem to be hints of yellow and orange. *Has my mind finally gone mad?* I stop and stare at the new sight for a few fleeting moments before deciding to make my way toward it. With every step, the colours begin to get more prominent, and before long they start dancing. *Is that...fire?* The thought breathes new life into my tired body. If there is a fire there must be people, people who can help me, people I can talk to.

I speed up, excited at the idea of not being alone. I attempt to call out, but my words get trapped in my throat. *How long has it been since I last spoke?* I clear my throat and try again.

"Hello," my voice is weak at first as my vocal chords try to remember how to work. "Hello? Is there somebody there? I am lost and need help."

Fog of the Lost
by Levi Hunstad-Neighbour

The fire of my salvation grows with every step, hoping for a response from the fog. A moment passes and I see a black figure appear in the swirling yellows and oranges.

"Hello, I see you, can you-" I stop as another figure appears, then another. I freeze as a chill runs down my spine. *I got too caught up in my own excitement, I didn't even think if they would be friendly.* The unknown shadows' movements are convulsive, with an unexpected fluidity. I stare toward the fire and start to speak but am cut off.

"you do not belong here, you are not one of usss!" an inhuman voice hisses from the fire, broken and piercing. The chill I experienced quickly turns to ice in my veins.

Suddenly, one of the shapes shrinks close to the ground and I hear the sound of running. The other two shapes follow with one seemingly staying upright. I turn and start to run, I don't have time to try and reorient myself, I just need to be away from here. I hear the figures start to call out, mostly broken words and guttural sounds, like a pack of animals signaling that there is food. The sounds of running get closer, I can't outrun them; they're too fast. I call for help, hoping there is someone who can hear me, something crashes into the back of my legs, toppling me over, and the cold hard ground approaches rapidly.

I hit the ground with a thud and feel the air leave my lungs. I don't have time to think. I turn over, my back to the dirt, as the creature crawls on top of me, striking at my body and head. I attempt to block the strikes as best I can, but then the others appear. Grabbing my arms, they pin me down as if they had practised this many times

Fog of the Lost
by Levi Hunstad-Neighbour

before. I finally get a good look at my assailants and see that they aren't animals, they're just like me, except... something was missing, something was off about their eyes. They looked cold and empty, missing some sort of humanity. The one on top of me reaches behind themselves and pulls out a weapon of some kind, I can't see it clearly through the darkness. It raises it into the sky... *This is it, this is my end,* I close my eyes and wait for the inevitable.

"**Hey!** Let them go." I hear someone behind me.
I open my eyes and see the assailants looking at the voice's origin, the weapon, which I now see is a makeshift knife, hovers inches from my face.
"I said let...them...go."

I see the knife begin to rise from my face, the creature's cold empty eyes staring forward, *"Now, this a surprissse, I did not think I would sssee one of you in our landsss."*
I hear something crash into the ground and take this time to look towards my saviour. The figure is half concealed by the fog's dense vapors, but I can see a bag sitting next to a pair of black combat boots. I look back to the creature on top of me and see it has cocked his head to the side, probably wondering what the figure was doing. Before either of us figures out what's happening, the sound of running can be heard and the hands holding my arms down start to let go.

A moment passes before I suddenly feel the weight on my body begin to lighten. I turn back to the creature with the knife and see the same black combat boot pushing its way deep into the creature's chest, forcing it off of my body, and tumbling along the dirt at my feet. The figure lands and in one fluid movement turns to the creature on my right, who has started to stand up and drives their fist directly into their forehead, sending the creature back down to the ground.

By now, I'm free from my constraints and crawl back a few feet, not wanting to get caught by a stray attack. I can't take my eyes off of the figure who I can now see more clearly. It was a woman with a muscular frame. The third creature was able to restrain her from behind, her crimson hair whips into the air as her foot comes down hard and her elbow makes impact with the creature's body. Her emerald eyes shone through the fog with an unbeatable determination. At this point, all three creatures had surrounded her and she stood, ready for anything.

"Can you stand?" her question was directed at me, even though her eyes were kept on her attackers.

"I think so," I respond, unsure if my adrenaline is numbing any pain.

"Good, then get up and get out of here."

Two of the creatures lunge at the mystery woman. She looks like she is dancing as she glides through the fog and contacts both of them, punching one away, while kicking the other into the air. I get up and stand dumbfounded at what I was witnessing. The knife-wielder is the last to approach, making an unbearable screech. The woman covers her ears and at this moment the last creature lunges with its knife.

Fog of the Lost
by Levi Hunstad-Neighbour

I don't realize it, but my body seems to move on its own, running toward the knife. *What am I doing? Am I trying to get myself killed?* The woman was still recoiling from the noise. *She's going to get hurt because of me, I'm not going to make it, what do I do?* My body is pushed to its absolute limit as I jump, attempting to get between the woman and the rapidly approaching weapon. *Come on, just a little further.*

Time seems to slow as the creature takes the last couple steps toward the woman, who isn't covering her ears anymore. Her hands make their way down hard into the creature's hands and arms, the knife coming loose from its grip. The woman slams her palm into the creature's face, causing it to stumble back. I hit the ground hard and see the woman spin around, her leg extending backwards as she kicks the final standing creature so hard it disappears into the fog. I lay on the ground and listen for the sound of any remaining creatures moving but there is only silence.

The woman exhales slowly, and I can hear her start to move. I sit up and look at her as she walks toward her bag which was a few feet to my left. I watch as she inspects the bag, then herself, before she puts the bag over her shoulder and begins walking into the fog.

"Wait. Thank you for saving me."

The woman stops her retreat and looks over at me, staring through me.

"Please, I...seem to be lost...can you help me? Do you know a way out of here?" The request ends up coming out more desperate than I want, but at this point any source of reassurance is needed.

Fog of the Lost
by Levi Hunstad-Neighbour

The mysterious woman takes a few moments before I see her take a step toward me, extending her scar covered hand. I take her hand and they feel rough and calloused as she pulls me up to my feet. Her piercing green eyes stare up into mine before she finally speaks.

"I think I know a way out, but I have been wrong before."

"Well, can I perhaps join you? I don't have much to offer but I will pay you back any way I can."

Taking a step back, she begins tapping a finger to her lips, parting them slightly, as she appears to be deep in thought. A few moments pass and it looks like she's about to speak before she silently shakes her head and taps her lips again. This goes on a few more times before she finally responds.

"I do not just team up with any stranger that I meet." She glides behind me as she speaks.

I turn to follow her voice and see her disappear into the fog as the last word leaves her lips.

"What is your name?" I hear from behind me in a hushed tone.

I whip around trying to find the source of the voice and see the emerald eyes slowly sink their way back into obscurity.

"Oh, my name is umm," for a moment I forget my name, unsure how long it has been since I had last used it.

"Your name is umm? Well, I suppose I have heard weirder ones," she retorts, her voice seemingly coming from nowhere and everywhere at the same time.

"N-no my name is Wesley; sorry, it's just been a while since anyone has asked fo-"

"It is fine Wesley, I am just trying to give you a hard time." Her eyes start to reappear once again seeming to part the fog as she re-approaches. "Well it is a pleasure to meet you Wesley, you can call me Morgan"

"It's nice to meet you Morgan... So does that mean you're willing to help me?"

"Well, since we are not strangers anymore," she says with a wink, "yes I suppose I can assist you out of this fog, just do not blame me if you dislike what you find once you are out."

Before I have the chance to respond Morgan grabs my hand, leading me into the fog.

"Let us get out of here before those things get up"

About a hundred steps go by before I finally break the silence.

"Hey Morgan, if you've left the fog, why are you here?"

"I am looking for something," Morgan says with such confidence it makes me question even asking her in the first place.

"Oh, well...have you found what you are looking for?" I hesitantly pry.

Morgan stops, turning her head to look at me "I guess we will have to wait and see Wesley. In all honesty, I do not know if I will be able to find what I am really looking for."

Unsure of what to say in response, I look down, avoiding eye contact.

Fog of the Lost
by Levi Hunstad-Neighbour

"Come on, let us get a little bit further before we stop and rest, I am sure we are both tired."

Morgan begins walking again, asking me questions about myself. I try to answer as many as I can, but the fog has taken a lot from me. I laugh when she tells me about the time she tried to prank her father but ended up being pranked herself. She asks me what my interests are and is shocked when I say creating stories. We go back and forth for a while before we finally stop to rest.

Together, Morgan and I gather wood and grass to make a fire in an attempt to fight off the cold. We keep the fire small, not wanting to get the attention of anything out in the fog. Morgan attempts to warm herself and sits next to the fire. I sit across from her and watch as she pulls something out of her bag.

"Are you hungry?"

"No, I'm ok, what is that?"

"Deer jerky, it's one of my favourite traveling snacks." She takes a big bite out of the dried meat and begins to chew. We sit in silence around the warmth of the fire, the pain pulsing through my body as the adrenaline wears off. I stare into the flame, and watch as the orange and yellow break the fog's gray curtain. A few moments pass before I finally speak up again.

"Why...did you save me?"

I watch as Morgan looks up from the fire and her glistening green eyes meet mine.

"Initially, it was because I cannot stand those creatures attacking anything. But once they were taken care of...it was your eyes."

"My eyes?"

"Yes, it was the look in your eyes. They seem so innocent, yet so full of life," Morgan looks away back into the fire, "they remind me of someone I used to know."

"What happened to them?"

"I do not know, they just disappeared one day. I searched for them for years until finally deciding to venture into the fog. Anyways, let us try and get some rest, we will need our strength if anything happens."

Morgan pulls her bag off her shoulder and lays it on the ground beside her.

"Goodnight Wesley." she lays down, using her bag as a pillow.

"Goodnight Morgan."

***

The fire is nothing but ash and smolder by the time Morgan wakes up. I don't know how long we have been resting but the pain from the attack is already starting to ease.

"Morning Morgan."

"Good Morning. Did you get any sleep last night?"

"Not really, I wanted to make sure nothing happened while we were resting, I figured we would want to be at one hundred percent before continuing."

"Well, let us get going, we have to get you out of this fog."

Fog of the Lost
by Levi Hunstad-Neighbour

Morgan sits up and stretches before she stands and gathers her bag. I stand and kick some dirt onto the last remaining embers of the fire. We begin walking and speak about what we are going to do once we are out of the fog. I tell Morgan about my dreams of adventure and love; she chuckles and tells me that she has seen enough adventures for one lifetime. We walk for thousands of steps talking and laughing. I was having so much fun with Morgan that I didn't realise that the fog is thin.

"Here we go Wesley, I got you out of the fog like you asked."
I look beyond Morgan and see it, the fog is parting ten, no twenty steps ahead of us. I look at Morgan and she is looking back at me, smiling.

"Well, what are you waiting for, get on out of here."
I take a few steps past Morgan, afraid of what is beyond the sea of gray I have known for so long.

"What about you? What are you going to do Morgan?"

"Well, I still need to find my friend."

I take a few more steps and see it - the land beyond the fog. I stand on the edge of the fog and look back to Morgan. She is fidgeting with her hair, looking back and forth between the fog and me. I reach out my hand and smile, "Morgan, do you want to come on an adventure with me?"

in sickness
by Elle Nyitrai

you take notice of a crimson stain
on the cuff of my left sleeve,
of the crescent moon indentations
at crossroads with my lifeline,
interlace tightly

when my black-biled nature
becomes evident at parties
take me home, tuck me in, text my mom
refuse my insistence on bearing it alone

though i ebb and flow, you chart my moons,
study the rhythm of my tides, of my breath,
my pulse, the twitch of my fingertips
allow my saltwater to pool in your collarbone

i make claims of burden and undeserving,
that there would be no grievances
should this be your grounds to leave
i apologize profusely, you say there is no need

even if just for tonight,

in sickness
by Elle Nyitrai

you could love me enough for the both of us
then in the morning, i will get up,
make the bed, you'll go to work,
leave breakfast on the nightstand

in sickness, you said
with time, become myself again
sanguine in the veins, grow back the flesh
in places where my melancholia was blood-let
so you can have and hold me in health

Strangling Blood Ties
by Chau Luong

Steam curls lazily from the pot as I stir the simmering sauce, encouraging the rich aroma of garlic and herbs to fill the air. My favourite playlist hums in the background, and I sway to the rhythm barefoot on the kitchen tiles, the soft clinking of my spoon against the pot keeping time. The late afternoon light filters through the window, golden and gentle, painting the scene in hues of quiet contentment.

My phone buzzes on the counter, and I let it vibrate away as I hum along to my favourite song. A second persistent buzz follows—unyielding. I reach for it with a lazy smile, excited at the thought of chatting with a friend.

The name on the screen stops me cold. My chest tightens and my pulse quickens, the serene beat of the music now drowning beneath the rush of blood in my ears.

The sweet yet short months of calm and freedom seem to unravel in a single breath, like a thread pulled too tight. My throat dries as I realize how deeply I have buried this feeling until it has clawed its way back, unbidden and unwelcome.

The phone buzzes again, insistent, and I freeze.

Laughs and high-pitched [jb2] shrieks reach the ceilings as your fast fingers prickle at my sides, tickling and occasionally nipping

Strangling Blood Ties
by Chau Luong

my skin in brief yet sharp and painful pinches. Tears breach my eyes as I cower over my sides, laughing uncontrollably.

"Love you, mama"

9

I swing forward a picture I drew of you and I, my smile competing in width with the printer paper. I showcase my work of art as my activity of the day in front of everyone.

"Look, mama. Happy birthday."

You take it into your hands as your friends congratulate me on my piece of art. You laugh, as you put it down.

"A better gift would be a bag. What would I do with this?"

10

The walls shake as we jump in excitement, screaming, "Thank you! Thank you! Thank you!"

We hold our new iPods in our hands, which are shaking with uncontrollable joy.

"Anything for you, my children."

11

The rock salt on the floor crunches slightly as my other knee shifts uncomfortably in its acquaintance. The numbness in my feet screams for movement almost as loud as my knees are screaming **fire**.

"I'm sorry, mama, we were bored at school and wanted to keep playing. I'm sorry, I won't do it again," I stifle between my cries. The tears are choking me up so much I'm almost unable to speak.

"Stop that. You're sorry? Wait until your dad gets home."

12

Strangling Blood Ties
by Chau Luong

Heat radiates off my skin like a furnace, and I feel paralyzed. I think it's the flu, but it feels like something more. My bed is a prison and simultaneously, my oasis.

Something cold touches my forehead, and I fight to open my eyes.

"Try to eat something, my child," you whisper as you pat the cold towel on my face.

Beside me, a hot bowl of rice porridge appears.

The chills shake my core, but I feel warm.

13

Giddiness runs up and down my spine as I swing open the front door.

"I got many awards at school today, mama!"

The TV plays on, unbothered, with the curtains drawn on a sunny afternoon in June.

"Mama, I got awards!"

...

...

...

"Mama?"

14

I stare blankly in disbelief.

"Show it to me."

You stand in front of the bathroom door, unmoving.

"But I told you, I am. I just put it on, why would I take it off just to show you? This is just weird. Let me out."

Strangling Blood Ties
by Chau Luong

Your scream rattles me to the bone, "Show me! Now!"

I stand frozen, unable to move.

"Why won't you show me! It's because it's true!"

"Mama, stop!"

The sharpness of the sound nearly matches the sudden sting that flares across my cheek-like a biting heat. My hand instinctively reaches for the raw and tingling skin, as if to search for the source of the taste of iron on my tongue.

You raise your hand again.

16

The air is thick in my lungs, and my mind buzzes incessantly. I need to let it all go. But I don't. I can't.

I'm finally alone in the illusory privacy of my bedroom, staring at the shards of glass splintered across the floor as it reflects the mess of me and what I've done.

The silence of the room is pressing in around me.

I kneel down, pulling a shard closer with the tip of my finger. It's cold.

I turn it in my hand, and it just stares at me, waiting.

I look down at my hands, still trembling, my nails digging into my palms.

I look back at the shard, and the desperation to bleed out my pain becomes unbearable.

16

I swallow hard, the lump in my throat rising with every shaky breath. My hands fumble as I tug the long sleeves over my arms, the soft fabric catching against the cuts and bruises that paint my skin. I bite the inside of my cheek, the sharp sting grounding me and the tears threatening to spill. My breath hitches as I smooth the sleeves down, willing myself not to look at the raw edges beneath.

Suddenly, I see myself cradled against the wall, shielding my head from your blows. I draw a deep breath.

The mirror catches my eye and I hesitate as my hand drifts to my hair, or more like what was left of it. I gather the uneven strands, feeling the ends where the scissors hacked through. The memory of your cold and furious grip flashes before my eyes. The back of my head suddenly aches as I remember how my head was yanked back, the metallic sound of the blades biting through echoing in my ears. I close my eyes against the image, but it clings to me, refusing to fade. All I see and hear are your new pet names for me.

Slut.
Whore.

With trembling fingers, I tie the remnants into a ponytail and try to smile like it doesn't matter. It is just hair.

I reach for the concealer, and my hands move on autopilot. Dabbing. Blending. Covering. The purples and blues slowly fade into a colour close enough to skin, but the face staring back at me is still a stranger. My thoughts can't help but recall every object, corner and surface that led to each dusky imprint. I press my lips together, my throat tightening. There is no use in crying; it won't fix anything. Maybe I needed to know what you would do if I did break the rules.

My reflection tells me I'm hollow. I wonder how long it has been since I'd smiled, really smiled.

Maybe it was the last time you told me you loved me. Maybe it was the last time I cared enough to follow your rules.

It doesn't matter how much it hurts. What does matter?

16

The water cradles me as its cool weight presses gently against my chest, rising past my shoulders and whispering over my ears. The world blurs into a muted silence, the faint hum of the bathroom fan fading beneath the steady rhythm of my heartbeat. The light above me dissolves into ripples of fractured silvery shadows.

For the first time, everything stops: the noise, the thoughts and the sharp edges of the world. There's a protest within my lungs, but I embrace the makeshift cocoon that I have made. I close my eyes and wait for the solace to become infinite.

A sudden and violent pounding against the bathroom door shatters my illusive utopia. The sound is like a thunderclap in my ears, distorted and magnified by the water, sending waves rippling around me. My body jerked upward instinctively, breaking the surface with a sharp gasp. Air forced its way into my lungs, heavy and oppressive.

17

The living room buzzed with voices and laughter, a chaotic warmth that used to feel like home. Balloons bob against the ceiling, their colors bright and mismatched, and the faint scent of vanilla cake mingles with the sharper tang of plastic streamers.

I lean against the doorway, clutching a cup of soda I don't want, offering a polite smile to anyone who glances my way. I *could've* said no, but that's not what sisters do; they show up because they *should*. My sister flits around the room, spilling over in little bursts as she leans into her friends' jokes. She looks older somehow, even though it has only been a few months since I last saw her.

I stay rooted to my spot, trying to ignore the familiar ache creeping in: the one that reminds me why I left and why coming back still hurts. Unfortunately for me, that ache has a face.

"Oh, so you *do* have time for your family."

There it is.

I bite my cheek and resist the urge to walk away.

"Hello to you too, ma."

I thought I had learned to drown out your cruel noise, but as I try to ignore the venom rolling off your tongue, rage boils in my veins.

That is it.

I turn my heel and move away. "I need to go home now."

Strangling Blood Ties
by Chau Luong

I flinch, the sharp sting of your fingers pinching the soft skin of my arm yanks me backward. My breath hitches as I turn to stare at you in disbelief.

"Listen when I'm talking to you!"

20

Each ring seems louder than the last, the sound reverberating in my skull relentlessly. The air suddenly became too thin, too sharp. The weight of the silence between rings presses heavier and heavier on me, filling the space with unspoken words I know I don't want to hear.

My thumb hovers over the screen, frozen between two options. It trembles as I urge it to make a decision.

And it does.

Car Rides
by Christina Jarmics

Let's take a car ride,
drive destinationless through
endless recurring roads and
fancy suburban neighbourhoods.

I will tell you my worries and woes
and you'll listen to mine.

This a silent stillness, to
the perpetually passing lights,
dusted dark alleyways, and
glistening glowing signs.

Illuminated the workers,
nighttime crawlers and us.

Slow turns,
winding roads and the
GPS turned off, as we
burn the midnight fuel
with heated breaths, and
drooping eyes.

Car Rides
by Christina Jarmics

bright lights dimmed as
dusk overtook the night,
stars hidden in glimpses between
the pollution pools,
giving us an idea of
how truly tiny we are.

Insignificant existence,
but with you, I don't feel so small.

I tell you my day with a
tightened chest that
methodically over time seems
to unwind.

You listen,
to your little girl speak,
bags pull at your eyes, beckoning
you for sleep.
Pain burns imaginary holes in your back,
and yet you listen.

Intently maneuvering,
shifting and turning,
watching my anxious expressions melt.

Car Rides
by Christina Jarmics

Sleep finds me easily those nights,
when we speak to each other,
basking in the beauty of the night.

Some nights,
the moon is not there,
we sit as silent still statues,
when tears prick your baby's eyes,
it was a rough day, but
you always make it better.

I wish one day,
to ask you the same question.
Key in hand,
morning buzz depleted and
evening snooze on the horizon.

That's when I'll ask,
as sun kisses moon goodnight,
with the same red puffy cheeks, and
sprung on you, out of the blue;

"Would you like to go for a ride tonight?"

The Expedition of Asbjørn Gunderson
by Levi Lewko

Day 0
Osnabrück, Capital of the Kingdom of Fjellnmark
    I was summoned to the Palace today by the Queen and her Ministers. Apparently, they've heard all about my expertise in the art of cartography! I've been offered payment of 10,000 krona to help lead an expedition exploring newly acquired territory in the Colonies! Finally, someone sees how talented I am!

Asbjørn Gunderson, 9th Jarl of Fubbarvik

Day 1
Osnabrück Harbour
    When I stepped out of my coach I was immediately overwhelmed by the stench of the harbour: a mix of salt water, fish, and sailors. I held my breath and paid the driver 2 krona to help carry my possessions to the ship which was anchored before us. It was a modest steam frigate, with small cannons protruding forth from its sides. The deck was broken up by stout smokestacks which puffed fumes between the masts and sails. The tallest of the masts flew the Kingdom's three-tailed naval ensign, a simple

The Expedition of Asbjørn Gunderson
by Levi Lewko

design of red, black, and gold. Next to my steam frigate was a merchant vessel. It hailed from a small city-state across the sea; some place I had only read on maps, some place called "the Free City of Snovburg".

I was shown to my quarters... and this has to be a joke! Someone of my status, noble birth, and education confined to a room smaller than a shoe box?! I hardly have room for all my bags, it is unacceptable and I will not stand for it...

I was just introduced to the Captain and the crew, a shiftier and more slovenly group of people, I have yet to meet. I was also informed that my cabin was "well above the size granted to most of the crew," and that, "if I continued to be ungrateful then I could sleep on the poop deck." I'm going to strangle that Captain in her sleep, I swear. To make things worse, I was also informed that there was no champagne on board. What the *fuck* am I supposed to drown my sorrows in? Rum? Like some kind of *commoner?* This is going to be a long boat ride.

Asbjørn Gunderson, 9th Jarl of Fubbarvik

Day 2
Middle of the Ocean

    I think I'm developing sea sickness; either that or it's the cook's deplorable food. You'd think that we would at least have a few good things to eat seeing as this is a government-funded voyage and all. But NOOOOO! That cheap ass Chancellor of the Exchequer had to pinch his krona's when it came to feeding us! I went to boarding school with that idiot. I know how badly he did in math class, why the Prime Minister appointed him is beyond me… The least he could have done was splurge on some goose and champagne!! But NOOOOO Asbjørn has to starve on board his floating tomb.

    And that's another thing! Who the hell named this hunk of scrap The Seagull? Nothing inspires elegance like a rat bird!

    I think I'm going to go scrounge around the pantry and find some weavel-less hardtack to gnaw on.

Asbjørn Gunderson, 9th Jarl of Fubbarvik and desperately hungry man

Day 3
(Sadly, Still) Middle of the Ocean

I think Captain Svensdötter can tell that all this time being cooped up is getting to me, she invited me to come play cards in her quarters with some of the other officers and important so-and-so's later tonight. These rubes don't know what they're in for; I'm quite the skilled card player, I'll probably beat them all without breaking a sweat!

That Captain is a liar and a cheat!!! She invited me into her room (which might I add is way grander than mine despite the fact I'm heading this expedition!) and took me for all I was worth! There's no way she could be that good, she must have cheated. I know. It was that first mate who she's weirdly close with! Or maybe it was all the watered-down brandy she served us. Yes, maybe she was trying to get me drunk so she could beat me at cards and win all the krona! Yes, that must be it, there's no way she's that good!

Asbjørn Gunderson, 9th Jarl of Fubbarvik and unlucky gambler

The Expedition of Asbjørn Gunderson
by Levi Lewko

Day 4
Deepsea

    Today was uneventful. I read a book and reviewed the crappy maps of the frontier again. How the Crown has managed to run a somewhat successful colony with this information is astounding. What's even more astounding is the fact that the Berlojans haven't annexed these territories from us yet, but I guess that's why I've been sent out.

Later, I walked about the deck of the ship and pretended I was back home in Osnabrück, strolling through Prince Munin Park. The smell of saltwater and the crying of the gulls ended the fantasy quickly.

Asbjørn Gunderson, 9th Jarl of Fubbarvik and salty sailor

Day 6
???

    The cabin fever has set in.

I am going mad.

        Nothing else of note.

Asbjørn Gunderson, 9th Jarl of Fubbarvik and madman

Day 8
Nyr Osnabrück, Capital of the Fjellnish Colonies

We docked in the colonial capital today around noon, I was ecstatic to finally see dry land and eat something resembling real food. I read all about this city and the Colonies when I was a boy, but I never imagined them to be so… provincial. The city (if you can even call it that) is tiny compared to its namesake, and aside from the Governor's home and a dozen administrative buildings, it's anything but grand. The vast majority of the buildings are minuscule, and as you get farther from the city centre they only grow smaller with less ornamentation.

When we departed I was informed that upon arrival in the Colonies, we would be greeted by a large welcoming committee and after a parade in our honour we would dine with the Governor. But when we pulled into port it was NOT what we were promised. I was expecting pomp and circumstance, not 100 or so middle-class burghers, waving flags on an <u>undecorated dock</u>!! After unloading our supplies from the steam frigate we were greeted by the Governor and his wife who had been in the pathetic crowd cheering our arrival. They were plain and both spoke with strong accents which are increasingly becoming a hallmark of being from the Colonies.

The Expedition of Asbjørn Gunderson
by Levi Lewko

The pair led Captain Svensdötter and me into a tacky open-top carriage which was PAINTED GOLD, not made of, painted. The Captain was overly nice to the Governor and his wife. "What a lovely welcome! You two are too kind! Really you shouldn't have." Lady, they waved flags at us and subjected us to the anthem being sung by an unprofessional school choir, we deserved better! The four of us rode through the city streets at a slow trot (I think one of the horses was lame). At one point the Governor's wife proudly mentioned how they had commissioned the carriage for our arrival. I informed her that in the Motherland members of the royal family and even the Prime Minister often ride in automobiles; she didn't talk to me the rest of the ride.

After an overly lengthy and awkward carriage ride, we arrived at the Governor's residence. It was a building that back in the Motherland would pass for a minor nobleman's auxiliary hunting lodge. We were treated to a large dinner of dishes, which I can only describe as a crude bastardization of the food in the Motherland.

During dinner, I was informed that tomorrow I would be introduced to a "Mr. Leif Anderson." Apparently, he's a fur trapper from the frontier who will be a guide on this expedition.

I think I drank a little too much, I'm beginning to fall asleep at my typewriter.

Asbjørn Gunderson, 9th Jarl of Fubbarvik and thoroughly underwhelmed

Day 9
The Governor's Home
Woe is me! I was informed this morning that we will be unable to bring all the things I've packed! The Governor has offered to keep them here in my guest room until the expedition is finished. Does that fool expect me to sleep on bedding that's under a thread count of 800 and bathe without my rubber duck while I'm in the WILDERNESS?!! I'll go look over all my things and try to find something I can part with; after that, we will be taken to board a train which will take us to the last major settlement in the frontier region.

We boarded the train around 2:00 pm and departed for Fort Fortinbras, the last spot of civilization before the area I am to map for the crown. The train ride was as underwhelming as the rest of this journey thus far; the landscape was pretty but I was sat next to a mother and her loud, weepy brat.
When we reached Fort Fortinbras, to say I was disappointed would be an understatement. This

place is nothing more than a sleepy hamlet encircled by a rotting wood palisade.
I was then brought to a very small cabin, or more appropriately a shack, where I was at last introduced to Mr. Leif Anderson. He's a man of about my age and height, with longer red hair and a matching beard. He appears to be quite strong. When we were introduced he was outside skinning a fox. I went to shake his hand and was mortified when he shook mine without first wiping away the blood!!
    The interior of his cabin was very… simpletons of taxidermy, a bit too much for my tastes. I can't believe I'm sleeping in here tonight.
I also can't believe that Mr. Anderson just told me to stop using the typewriter because he is trying to sleep, the nerve!

Asbjørn Gunderson, 9th Jarl of Fubbarvik and so very disappointed

Day 10
Fort Fortinbras, edge of the Fjellnish Colonies
    Mr. Anderson woke me at the crack of dawn today; It took him a few tries to fully rouse me. After a bland and flavourless breakfast, I was put to work packing the covered wagon we would be travelling together in. When my bags alone

ended up taking up half of the space, Mr. Anderson yelled at me.

"What the hell are you doing city boy? We need that room for supplies like food and water!"

Such a simpleton, he doesn't understand the comforts of civility. I acquiesced to leaving some more things behind at his cabin to make room for "supplies" after he threatened to leave me alone when we got out there in the wild. I only have 3 outfits now, I hope he's happy! We then departed town and I waved goodbye to the civilized world.

I miss my typewriter already.

While we were leaving Mr. Anderson asked if I knew how to use a firearm. At first, I assumed he was just teasing me because of my noble upbringing. I told him how I go hunting for pheasants and elk every fall and waited for a snarky reply. However, he responded that it was a good thing as there had been rumours in Fort Fortinbras. Rumours of raiding parties being sent from the Colonies of the Tsardom of Berloja to stop our colonial expansion. He seems worried we will run into one of these parties on our journey.

Asbjørn Gunderson, 9th Jarl of Fubbarvik and quite anxious

Day 14
Wilderness

We've travelled 15 km in the past two days. Heading west, we entered into a dense wood which stalled our progress. It got so dense in fact that we had to stop, Mr. Anderson said he could cut down a few trees to open our path up again. He forced us to make camp for the night. He cooked us some kind of canned meat, it wasn't good. I failed to pitch my tent, Mr. Anderson asked if I needed help but I refused, I'll just sleep under the collapsed tent.

I admit, the shadows of these woods are playing with my mind, I can't sleep and keep seeing things.

Asbjørn Gunderson, 9th Jarl of Fubbarvik and scared explorer

Day 17
Wilderness

While going to the bathroom today I accidentally used poison ivy. I have been scratching my backside nonstop for hours and Mr. Anderson hasn't stopped laughing. That oaf could have told me that it was poison ivy when he watched me grab it to take to our latrine!

Asbjørn Gunderson, 9th Jarl of Fubbarvik and itchy

Day 20
Wilderness

It took more days than expected to clear the way through the woods and Mr. Anderson tired himself out doing so. He now expects me to unload the supplies when we make camp tonight.

We ended up travelling about 5 km out of the woods today. There is a great plateau of rolling hills and patches of trees, just on the other side of the forest. I have decided to name it Helgasland after our dear Queen, the woman who sent me out to this place, perhaps as punishment.

Asbjørn Gunderson, 9th Jarl of Fubbarvik and potentially exiled explorer

Day 29
Helgasland

We have travelled about 100 km in the past few days, the terrain has been gradually getting hillier. It's also clear that winter is coming, when we left camp today the ground was frosty and I had to pull out my great coat. Nonetheless, my map is coming along swimmingly.

Mr. Anderson is such a good listener! Sometimes I think I might be annoying him with all my talking, but he hasn't told me to shut up yet.

Asbjørn Gunderson, 9th Jarl of Fubbarvik and very cold

Day 35
Helgasland

    Mr. Anderson told me to shut up! We sat in silence for a while after that. Eventually, Mr. Anderson broke the silence by apologizing; he asked me to keep telling my story.

Asbjørn Gunderson, 9th Jarl of Fubbarvik and chatterbox

Day 36
Helgasland

    While on the road today I asked Mr. Anderson about his life. He seemed surprised and enthused that I was interested in listening to him talk for once. He told me that his family were some of the pioneers who founded Fort Fortinbras. When he was a teenager he began to hunt for pelts that he sold to merchants who would turn them into luxuries back in the Motherland. He joked that maybe my fur hat was once an animal he'd shot. He also told me that he has ventured into Helgasland many times, just never this far, but he always liked to call it Leif's Land. I don't know why but I like it a bit more.

Asbjørn Gunderson, 9th Jarl of Fubbarvik and enjoyer of fur hats

Day 48
Helgasland

    We crested a hilltop today and in the distance saw a range of gorgeous mountains which I named Ragnarr's Range, after our studious King Consort.

    After setting up camp Leif went out for a bit to hunt us some fresh meat for dinner. While he was gone I attempted to set up our tents to surprise him, while putting mine up I accidentally caused a support pole to snap and tear the fabric. When Leif returned he wasn't as mad as I expected, he said I'll just have to sleep in his tent. With how cold it's getting it might not be the worst, from a strictly utilitarian point of view of course.

Asbjørn Gunderson, 9th Jarl of Fubbarvik and Leif's tentmate

Day 55
Helgasland

    I dropped my mirror while fording a creek yesterday. Leif offered to help me shave, I'm very glad he has a steady hand.

Asbjørn Gunderson, 9th Jarl of Fubbarvik and well shaved

Day 60
Helgasland

Leif asked me about what life is like in the motherland. I told him all about it, he wants to see it. I promised that I'd show it to him someday.

Asbjørn Gunderson, 9th Jarl of Fubbarvik and Leif travel agent

Day 66
Helgasland

Leif got bit by a snake today while trying to fix part of the wagon, he hacked the thing to bits with his knife. I had to suck the venom out, I had no clue what I was doing but Leif stayed calm.

Asbjørn Gunderson, 9th Jarl of Fubbarvik and medic

Day 70
Helgasland

We have nearly reached Ragnarr's Range, when we got to the top of a hill we found a picturesque lake. Leif thinks it would make the perfect spot for a city someday, I agree with him. I added it to my ever-growing map. We will make camp early and set out tomorrow to reach the mountains.

Asbjørn Gunderson, 9th Jarl of Fubbarvik and excited explorer

Day 72
Helgasland

We were packing up camp yesterday when we heard a noise from a nearby hill. There was a group of 4 horsemen in green uniforms, flying the flag of Berloja. Leif grabbed his rifle and I drew my pistol, we tipped our table and used some of our supplies to hastily build a barricade. He told me that he wanted me to keep my head down and not get shot. I heard the thunder of the horses and the guns firing. A bullet tore through the table just next to my head and I instinctively let out a yelp. Leif turned to see if I was all right and at that moment a bullet tore into his chest, sending out a shower of blood. My adrenaline kicked in and I rose from the table wildly firing my pistol into the only remaining horseman who fell from his steed, dead like his comrades.

I knelt over Leif, my eyes tearing up and my hands shaking. After a few moments of silence, I quietly leaned in and hugged his bloodied body. It was at this moment that he let out a cough, the shot wasn't fatal. I was so relieved I kissed him.

Asbjørn Gunderson, 9th Jarl of Fubbarvik

Day 75
Helgasland

    Leif seems to be recovering well, I think that in a few days, he will be good enough to travel again.

Asbjørn Gunderson, 9th Jarl of Fubbarvik and cautiously hopeful

Day 80
Shores of Lake Leif

    I buried Leif today

renaissance man
by Elle Nyitrai

a da vinci reincarnate, my boy
passion for workings of body and mind,
humanist dedication to achievements of man
particularly, his own
she watched him sketch his self portrait as vitruvian
time is yet to teach the era of romantics
a renaissance man indeed
she cannot decide whether to cry out
too much or not enough, what does it matter
tears of either made of the same saline
unaware he made a better muse than lover
willing to become a cadaver for her da vinci
cold and anatomical, worth his study
scientific method for self discovery
required repeated experimentation
pompous mirage, opaque to another woman
she takes cruel comfort in the thought that one day
he'll leave her too, neither of us immortalized
because he needs no mona lisa
when his canvas is his reflection
his mirror, his magnum opus
hours when her mind craved sleep

renaissance man
by Elle Nyitrai

spent at the window, on her knees, satisfactory
she's galileo searching constellation confirmations
and singling out stars to beg for
a heavenly body he'd be dedicated to
yet renaissance men disprove universal truth,
with fate in skies, she can be a logician too
so when the masculine sun claims heliocentricism
i will no longer play the reflective moon

Only Monster
by Teresa Anderson

"Don't go in the water."

The only warning that Siobhan gave.

Water.

Did she forget that Liam had spent three years in the worst of the waters with U-boats? And they said his mind was fraying.

He took the same path as always, but his legs were not as limber as they used to be. Each trip took a little longer than the one before it. He did reach the water, though. A stretch of blue more exquisite than the ocean, for Loch Ness offered a sense of peace.

They said a monster dwelled within. Some still say it. Fools.

After the war, Liam had reunited with an old friend, an American, who'd brought back photos.

"Enough," Liam had said after witnessing another pit of emaciated, partially burned corpses.

Peter pocketed the rest. "Sorry. Sorry." He reached for his ale, but his hand shook. His forehead sunk to his palm, elbow on the scratched table. "I tried to feed one. A little boy. But my rations were too rich, and I didn't think of that, and he..." Peter trailed off, and covered his face.

"It's not your fault." Liam tentatively reached beyond the ale, clasping Peter's elbow. "You hear me? It's not your fault."

Peter wiped his eyes. "We killed them."

Yes, when Liam had first learned of Dachau, he'd heard of the retribution on the SS, too.

"Good," said Liam, simply.

"Is it?" Peter lifted his head. "They were unarmed, and they begged, but we killed them anyway. And it felt good, so doesn't that make me a murderer like them?"

Liam stared for a moment. "No." His focus dropped to the concealed photographs, the starving dead in Peter's jacket. "It doesn't."

Now, Liam found his spot, the grass worn thin by his visits. Siobhan would gripe about the mud on his trousers, but if he gave her a kiss after, all would be fine.

Fine, that was what the world was supposed to have become.

Never again, they said. Never would people be so cruel.

But it did happen again. And again. And again.

The Troubles in Northern Ireland; the Years of Lead in Italy; residential schools in Canada; race riots in the States; wars in Vietnam and Korea; genocides in Pakistan and Cambodia. Just this morning, the news was filled with pictures of the ongoing slaughters in Rwanda.

Liam closed his eyes, inhaling the cleansing scent of pine. Water splashed his outstretched legs.

He opened his eyes and smiled.

Eyes in the water became a large head, attached to a long neck.

Her size always astounded him, but it was her gentleness that eased the cracking emptiness inside.

She nuzzled his coat pocket.

"Yes, I brought 'em." He pulled out the candies and unwrapped one. Gnarled knuckles made it difficult, but she was patient. The whisky-flavoured ones were her favourite, his too, and they snacked together as the evening sun painted the water in golden hues.

After enjoying her treats, she curled her neck around him, a gentle hug, and rested her head next to his thigh. Leaning against the strong muscles of her neck, he settled in.

It was here that the doubt stopped festering. While decades of memories, flashes of suffering swam in his mind, he would find himself reduced to the realization that there was no God. How could there be when such unrelenting horror ran rampant? Or maybe, God had abandoned them for that reason.

But here, in moments like this, mystical benevolence existed. Here, he could believe that there might be something better besides cold darkness when Death came for him, for Siobhan. Something better that must have greeted Peter after he'd tied that rope around his neck. And something better that must have embraced all those innocents surrounded by hate, abuse, Zyklon B, fire, machetes, or bullets.

Nessie was asleep, her light snoring akin to soft humming.

"You're not a monster," he whispered. "We are."

If I am the moon, then you are the sun
by Emma Marion

Glistening rays of light dancing
elegantly down from the sky,
Your warmth and love spreading around for all to feel.
My cold glare from the night sky will never meet yours,
Never get to bask in your glow
and feel your touch upon me.
Your beams so bright, hiding in an unfamiliar bliss.

If I am autumn, then you are spring.
Opposites in their own ways, never fitting together truly,
You, the rosy dawn of life and new beginnings.
Me, the dusk of death, bringing upon withering leaves,
Animals flee me to escape an oncoming frost.
They flock to you and frolic amongst flowers and sun.

If I am the land, then you are the sea.
An unexplored vastness I only wish I could know,
Opposing rough and gentle waves crashing against me,
Slowly eroding and chipping away with your touch.
Losing a piece of myself every time we meet,
But never desiring our dance together to dissolve.

If I am the moon, then you are the sun
by Emma Marion

If I am a weed, then you are a flower.
Your petals delicately dancing in a soft breeze,
So vulnerable in the garden, eye-catching and carefree.
Dragged down by my grasp, reaching out to hold you,
My prickles and leaves entangling you in desperation.
Your allure is addicting, and I am absorbed in it with awe.

If I am the end, then you are the beginning.
You sow the very seeds of creation itself,
Without you, there is nothing and I am extinct.
I bring about a final conclusion, something to avoid,
A darkness to snuff out your glowing presence.
I cherish your handiwork as I huddle in your shadow.

I want to capture smells
by Mel Perez

It's been five days
My suitcase sits lazily
Taking up my favourite corner
Clothes volcano out
Messy and thrown...again
They...
Smell like them.
Smells like the home they effortlessly made for me.
Pants smell like the couch I sat on while we ate 7/11 chicken strips.
This white stained tee, which I wore while we slept next to each other.
Brown-stained socks from midnight walks in mysterious dirt
We didn't give a wink too.
Smothering each other with our past, late-night sonnets we sighed sharing with each other.
I wonder if the sky sighed the same.
Floral patterned pyjama pants from our overcooked night
They wanted to steal.
I would let them.

Her black hoodie

I want to capture smells
by Mel Perez

Messy & thrown on bleach
Perhaps another midnight art project
Floral embroidery crossing over hearts.
Collection of her life, memories,
Now, a collection of my dried mucus and cries
Collected on a plane ride to an unfamiliar home.

***

It's been 41 days.
I've made progress
One neglected jacket escaped the case
Scents barely lingering outside the front staircase
Now, tossing in bubbles
Cleansing a memory out.
Perhaps it was that seven am walk to the dentist.
Waiting along the beach, waiting again.
Collecting more scents
Air thickened by my overlapping thinking traps.
You seemed to avoid all too well.

It's now been 75 days.
I'm prolonging their release.
I don't want to unpack
I don't want to unpack my clothes
I don't want to unpack their smells
Or wash the memories out.

I want to capture smells
by Mel Perez

I want to capture them.
Until I see them again
Where smells can harbour every thread
Not a worry to steam.
Their air will soon seep between the seams.

Save Me a Seat
by Rachel Fitzgibbon

I say I'll meet you there
And ask you to save me a seat
I know I'm late, but I'm on my way
I promise I'm just down the street

Yet when I arrive at the venue
There's standing room only
No seat has been saved
So I'm left ignored and lonely

I justify that it would have been rude
To hold up a chair
I ignore that it stings
To think that they didn't care

That they are not bothered
That I'm standing alone
Pushed to the outskirts
And left again on my own

My whole life's been spent
Looking in from outside

Save Me a Seat
by Rachel Fitzgibbon

Connections evade me
And I can never tell why

From cliques and new groups
To friends and acquaintances
It seems that every time I try
To form new relationships
I am doomed to fail

Out on the playground
I made up games just for one
And twenty years later
I'm still left out of the fun

Inside jokes I don't get
And to events uninvited
It's been like this so long
I can barely feel slighted

I've changed what I wear,
What I eat, what I say
But I'm still left behind
And I'm starting to fray

Is habitat innate,
Or is it created

Save Me a Seat
by Rachel Fitzgibbon

Am I born to be lonely,
And my heart left deflated

Or do we adapt into it,
After years left behind
Since my soul is too weary
And I just feel resigned

Have I brought this upon myself?
All my efforts been wasted?
Or am I really so bad
You'd rather I stay away instead

I know I say the wrong things
And stay in my shell
But I'm trying so hard
And I'm not doing well

I know that I'm odd
I'm ill-fitted and strange
But that doesn't mean
I deserve to be estranged

So, I'm telling you now
I'm on my way there
I'll be there so soon

Save Me a Seat
by Rachel Fitzgibbon

I swear, I swear

So please, please, please
If nothing else, and nothing more
Just save me a seat
(or at least some space on the floor)

Daydreams
by Dovonna Meloche

I imagine eyes that make me feel at ease.
I imagine a smile as warm as the sun.
Gray mirrors that reflect devotion,
lips that taste like peace.

I imagine lazy morning communions in this cathedral of our own making.
I imagine a laugh that makes my chest bloom.
Cups of black coffee sweetened by "I love yous."
Fingers that get caught in the tangles of my hair.

I imagine tender-firm hands and tender-firm kisses.
I imagine a voice-like silk ribbons around my wrists.
And skin that smells of home.
Quiet giggles and breathless sighs.

But these dreams and imaginings of a life not meant for me
Will stay a dream.
An elusive possibility of you and me that I convinced myself was destiny.
Now just silly make-believe, a stupid, *stupid*, fantasy.

Part Three:
VISIONS

A Spiraled Journey
by Franz Valencia

Jaunty music was the first thing I noticed. It filled the air like a physical thing, condensed in a small room, reverberating in my skull and filling my chest. Bells and whistles and other such instruments chirped and trilled. Beneath it all, there was the rustling of wind and the whining of an engine.

The second was the seat. Slightly warm, and yet draped in my clothes, it felt like a strange nirvana. Gravity pulled me deeper into the seat, heavy and smothering and warm, deep enough until it felt like I would become one with it. On my cheek, I could feel the cold plane of a glass window and I clung to the feeling like a lifeline.

It took heavy effort to not fall into sleep's embrace once again. I blinked, lethargic and slow. My eyelids felt like they had been peeled back, behind my head, and farther still until my eyes grew a shivering cold. I could barely remember anything beyond the moment. Could barely think, my mind under a thick miasma that filtered each thought through a distorted lens and churned out sludge. A heavy, cloying scent was in the air, trapped as it was in the small expanse, so pungent I wanted to puke.

I shifted from where I slept and glanced forward. Grey and black shadows in every corner, and a beaming yellow light, greeted me. My friends were there and they laughed, smiling. One, I could not see, driving. The other looked at me and the person-shaped thing to my

A Spiraled Journey
by Franz Valencia

right. I was too out of it to look right. Their faces were blurred, but I recognized them well enough. I tried to smile and they laughed harder. The music kept blaring; it was almost overwhelming. Just like the light.

The cold plane of glass shook me of my reverie. The contrast between the cold in my head and the warmth everywhere felt like a constant lure into sleep's embrace. I blinked, feeling lethargic and slow.

I shifted from where I had slept and glanced forward. A blurring of colors, of grays and yellow hiding in the corners greeted me. My friends were there and they were laughing. One, who I could not see, was driving. The other looked at me and the person-shaped thing at my side. I was too out of it to look right. Their faces were featureless and eyeless, but I could see their smiles and recognized them well enough. I tried to smile in return and they laughed harder. The music continued blaring; it was almost overwhelming. Just like the light.

The cold woke me. I blinked, feeling lethargic and slow. I shifted from where I had slept and glanced forward. Gray and yellow turning green, a blurring of color that framed my vision greeted me. My friends were there and they laughed, smiling. One, I could not see. The other looked at me and the person-shaped thing to my right. I didn't want to look right. I tried to smile and they laughed harder. The music continued blaring. The light was overwhelming.

The cold bit me. I blinked. I glanced forward. A rainbow of colors greeted me, trapping my vision and dragged my eyes to look forward. My friends laughed. I don't recognize them. They looked like flesh pretending to be human. One looked at me and to my right. I was too terrified to look right. They laughed harder. The music and the light were too overwhelming.

Ice shards shaved my brain. My eyelids moved, up and down. I was terrified but something compelled me to glance forward. A kaleidoscope of colors, beyond the rainbow, stared at me in all wave-patterns. Something laughed. It was an alien shaped thing that wasn't alive. Something next to me giggled. A melody repeated itself, each note distorted and stretched long and longer until it became an otherworldly spiral. The light roared. I needed to get out.

The thought slithered its way into my head and lingered like a serpent, constricting my head and squeezing until it was the only thought left. I needed to get out. I had to get out. To run, to flee, to escape, to scurry to fly to crawl to slither to get out and away from here, away as far as possible, anywhere but here, away away away but I was trapped. There's no way out and the shadows knew and they laughed and laughed and laughed as the rainbow danced, always dancing forever dancing as the heat and the cold ripped me apart and put me back and there's no way out.

The sequence repeated itself. Reality faded into a repeating pattern, a series of endless loops that got worse and worse. Time was long gone. Merciless cold, the laughter of things beyond comprehension, and the clarion chime of hell. Each time the light got brighter. I smiled every time.

A Spiraled Journey
by Franz Valencia

And then finally, mercifully, the light outgrew everything, even the sequence, and devoured me.

An eternity of nothing passed. I blinked. A different warmth surrounded me, but flickering like a dying flame. I could hear the crackling of fire. There might have been shouting or some other sound, but I couldn't tell.

With great effort, I forced myself upright from where I laid. Darkness greeted me, held back only by hungering flames that surrounded me and bled the world in reds and black. Howling winds whipped my ears and threatened to strip what little heat that warmed me from the fires. In front of me laid a ruined wreckage of steel, a cairn made of destruction. I didn't see anyone else.

A haziness still held me in its grasp, that forced me to drag my thoughts to think. The cold in my head had been drained out and replaced with a warm sensation that pooled in what remained. Gingerly, I reached and touched the back of my head and pulled back, feeling something wet and sticky.

In the light of dancing flames, I saw something red in my hand.

Oh, I thought. For once, my mind had cleared, if only briefly. This isn't good. It was the only thought I had before the cold crawled over me despite the warmth of the fire. I shivered, but when I tried to stand, a wave of dizziness came over me before a sudden lance of agony punctured my leg and I stumbled back, once again sitting.

The pain wrapped itself around my leg, crushing, and the wind and the cold left me shivering as it embraced. All I could do was

A Spiraled Journey
by Franz Valencia

lie back down. Lie back down and close my eyes, letting the cold sink me into deeper and deeper darkness. Until everything turned black.

Then ice tore its way through my subconsciousness, pulling me, dragging me out of sweet darkness. My soul wished to scream but could not, trapped in Samsara. I blinked. I glanced forward.

The cycle repeated itself.

The Script
by Myra Monday

Stick to the script
It tells you what to do
I'll say this
You'll say that
A ping pong of pleasantries
Always knowing the next move
As it is a pre written conversation
One so structured and secure
Yet so easy to slip
Like walking on the edge of a cliff
No guard rail to help
Only you and your balance
Doing your best to not fall off
But no matter how hard you try
It's hard to stay up
When the wind is always pushing you around
As people are so uncertain
Always trying to throw you off your path
And you can't plan the conversation
If you don't know what they'll say next
"Just move with the conversation" they say
When they don't know how hard that is

The Script
by Myra Monday

As it was something never taught
It has no rules, no specific way
That's why I have a script
Usually filled with observing silence
So I know how you will respond
If I ever have something
I'm not too scared to say

Purple Loosestrife Invasion
by Brennan Kenneth Brown

Lythrum salicaria: six-petaled nobility,
  purple-blooded & beautiful, arrived
  uninvited to these shores. The settlers
  called it "purple plague" but secretly
  admired how it made wasteland look wealthy.

Each flower a tiny crown, imperial & unapologetic.
Funny how a thing can be both—
  invasive & lovely. GIS maps of stolen treaty land rendered
  in elegant AutoCAD. How I take up space in academia
  with my articles on decolonization written in perfect MLA.

The wetland ecologist measures
  displacement by volume: One plant produces 2.7 million seeds annually,
  Each one the size of grinding poverty. Each one carrying the genetic
  memory of how to outlast winter. Scatter-shot survival strategy.

In riparian zones where cattails once filtered water pure,
  this European beauty spreads her royal authority.
  Indian Status Card lists both English & French names.

Purple Loosestrife Invasion
by Brennan Kenneth Brown

Naturalists marvel at the mechanics
of domination: how it forms geometric
monocultures, eradicating previous growth patterns.
The way my tongue wraps around academic jargon,
stumbles on Michif pronunciation, language loss a kind of density gradient.

Each August, the Red River's banks light up like bruised sunset.
Even the conservationists pause before pulling it up by the roots.
The way scholarship committees photograph yr face for EDI reports.

The biology of belonging gets complex:
rhizome systems below ground create labyrinthine networks,
each node a colonial outpost. We persist in marginal zones.

To remove it, they've imported European beetles,
fighting invasion with invasion.
Catalogue genetic markers for authenticity.

Survival means learning to thrive in disturbed soil.
& the only way forward is to become what they never expected:

A wetland full of purple fire. A catastrophic abundance.
A mixed-blood scholar writing herself into existence—

Purple Loosestrife Invasion
by Brennan Kenneth Brown

despite every attempt at ecological control. Watch me bloom
in the margins.

Conservationists say each flower can self-pollinate,
    carrying forward its own continuation. Call it hybrid vigor.
    Call it genocidal gardens.
    Call it the inevitable price of purple-petaled persistence.

At night I dream in infrared: heat signatures of refugee species
    finding home in unfamiliar waters.
    Red River knows our names, holds our history in her silt.
    She doesn't care what genus claims these banks,
    only that we learned to root deep & flower fierce

despite everything.

I Love You
by Christina Jarmics

"Do you love me?"

elegant words etched onto paper,
meaningless moments conjured up
in a dreamer's sleepless mind

diligently, delicately typed
the glaring glossy screen met her eyes,
reading along as thoughts became fiction.

Those few words softly interrupted the calm quiet night as a girl looked behind her

peering eyes positioned around,
eagerly listening to the
new blood speak

poets and writers,
well-versed in literature.

It was there I uttered those words,
more than a year ago.

I Love You
by Christina Jarmics

surrounded by those much better at prose,
metaphors elegantly written, recited with ease.

And yet, a platform given,
from where my trembling hands held my phone,
as I continued.

A boy stared down at the girl

each writer was different,
diversities and identity seeped
throughout the room.

in a sea of brilliant bright lights,
only one blinded me,
drawing myself to its intoxicating flame.

His eyes locked onto hers and for a moment everything went still.

glancing eyes caught each other,
linking and connecting, moments
at a time, before they
drifted apart. But
pulling each other back together
mere seconds later

I Love You
by Christina Jarmics

a beat red girl and melting boy.

His body slumped into the couch,
engulfed by the disgustingly printed seats.

"how can a man such as myself not love the night sky when stars shine around it? How can I not be warmed on the coldest nights by the beauty of the moon?"

each ended sentence,
guided glance,
serenaded you unintentionally.

your body pooling
filling into the felt cushions,
unearthed an unknowing desire,
for me to join you,
melt, mix and muddle.

fleeting feelings,
common with bursting bladders.
butterflies dancing in guts,
mistaken for social anxiety.

It was hours later
when I realized

I Love You
by Christina Jarmics

"But, do you love me?"

words previously interrupting the
autumn writing club night.
Were words etched into my soul,
and meant for you.

Fiction became reality,
sliding dm's became dinner,
and these words,
became ours;

"I do not just love you; I need you. Like the waves in the ocean need the moon, the cattle need water, I need you. You are my ground, air in my lungs, the fire in my chest. Every day I'm without you, is like the morning without the sun, meaningless."

Small Joys
by Chau Luong

The silky-smooth notes of the trumpet flows along the cool air of the fans and washes over the steering wheel. Small joys, they say. I've found mine in mindless cruises along the outskirts of the city. My fingers tap the edge of the wheel, keeping up with the beat, as though I'm part of the band.

A black-and-white cruiser emerges as its red and blue lights flash my rearview mirror. My eyes are captivated by the demanding neon flashers behind me, racing closer. The blaring siren competes with the jazz music, but the thundering pulse in my ears wins the battle. The world blurs into a frenetic dance of heightened colours and slowed movements. I feel my mouth dry with a lingering taste of copper. Each inhale stings like a gulp of icy air.

Shit. Shit. *Shit*.

What's going to happen next? What am I going to do next? They always say to stay calm and follow the police officer's instructions.

I would do that, of course. I would pull over. I would follow the police officer's instructions. I would not make a scene. I would be smart about it, of course. I *will* be smart about it. I won't be the next case on the news. I refuse to be.

Small Joys
by Chau Luong

I swerve to the side of the road, gravel spraying in all directions as I skid to a stop. The marked vehicle mirrors my sudden halt, a predatory shadow in my rearview. Keep your hands on the wheel, they say. I preemptively roll down my window and position my palms to rest flat on the face of the steering wheel, sweat instantly melding with the leather. The irritation in my eyes from the salt of my sweat begs me to move my hands, but I blink through the pain.

The crunch of gravel boots echoes with each step, drawing closer, steady and deliberate. The intense glow of the patrol car's lights reflects off my rearview mirror, a red and blue heartbeat that pulses in rhythm with the tightness in my chest. The officer's silhouette shifts slightly with every step, a hulking, deliberate shape against the glare of the setting sun.

A sharp tap cuts through the suffocating silence, and my breath hitches. As I turn my head, I meet the stern gaze of a police officer who looms over me like an unrelenting storm. My fingers fumble for the button, and the window lowers in a hesitant whir.

"What brings you out here?"

The first question. I part my lips to answer, but the dryness in my throat makes me lose the function of my voice. I struggle to make a sound, but I am left staring dumbfoundedly at the officer. Without a response, I'm suspicious. Say something. Do something. *Be* innocent. I attempt to convey innocence through a slight shrug of my shoulders.

Small Joys
by Chau Luong

"License and registration, *now.*"

The authoritative demand cuts through the tension in the air and as each second passes, it only thickens with uncertainty. I slowly nod, my movements deliberate, and extend my hand toward the glove compartment. My fingers brush the handle for a mere second before I hear the most dreadful sound.

Click

My heart lurches as the metallic sound echoes in the confines of the car.

"Hands where I can see them!" The officer's voice explodes like a sudden thunderclap that rattles my resolve. My hands shoot out of the window like a reflex, the officer's eyes boring into mine. Sweat beads off his furrowed brow, creating a rivulet of tension that mirrors my own.

"Out of the car now!"

The rapid drumming of my pulse reverberates through every inch of my body, almost jumping out in dissonant fear. Time itself has shifted into overdrive, and my senses are on high alert, catching even the faintest tremor in the air. My heart, an erratic drum, thunders in

Small Joys
by Chau Luong

my chest, its rapid beats syncing with the chaos unfolding around me. Comply, every rational fiber screams. I should comply. I need to comply, but a chilling uncertainty roots me in place, an unwilling participant in this twisted dance.

    Follow the officer's instructions.
    Right. That's all I have to do. I swallow hard, my throat tight, and reach for the door handle.

    BANG!

    The metallic tang of fear clings to my tongue, and my breaths come in shallow gasps; the rhythm is disrupted by the erratic drumming of my heart. I glance at my trembling hands, the skin pallid, veins pulsating visibly. A persistent, high-pitched ringing in my ears drowns out the world. I could be dead.
    The piercing whine feels like a thousand needles, pricking at the edge of my consciousness. As I struggle to catch my breath, I take one more glance at my rearview mirror to find the police car still racing closer with its lights flashing. I gently press my foot on the brakes and steer towards the shoulder of the road. As I slow to a stop, the ringing starts to recede, like a tide pulling away from the shore. I observe the approaching marked vehicle as the retreating ringing leaves behind a faint echo, a ghostly reminder of its presence. The cruiser weaves around my stopped vehicle, gravel spraying up from its tires. Relief fills my lungs and I utter a sigh. I watch the receding lights until they

Small Joys
by Chau Luong

become a distant speck, the mundane road once again stretching out before me. The tranquil sound of the saxophone emerges from the faint echo of the intrusive ringing and its smooth tones weaves a tapestry that wraps around me once again. I lean my head back against the headrest to allow the tension that had gripped me to dissipate like morning mist. I could've been dead.

Small joys, they say.

Building in Dead Sands
by Morgan McLean-Alexander

Storm clouds were built up like thorny hedges, violent waves of black blue crashing upon the rocky shore. Light burst in the distance, a fire shooting up to the cloudy sky and burning a longboat to smithereens. On the shore people screamed internally, no cries were heard aloud for it was considered insolent to the emboldened dead to cry at their funeral. No one dared to even sniffle, when without a hint of warning a scream erupted, though a battle horn had been blown at a feast. Shivers climbed the spines of the brave and scared fellows on the shores, for all knew the source but had never heard her bellow like that before.

It was not the scream of a woman, nor the scream of a man. But the aching cry of a forlorn girl. At least in that moment, that is how Skal Palesign felt. Felt as though they were a useless, agitated girl; who wasn't wearing the proud jacket of her father upon her shoulders; wasn't standing in the middle of her men and fellows. She wasn't hearing the angered roar of their few dragons above; and wasn't realizing they just inherited the position of Reignherus. She was just a girl right then, crying in grief for her father whose remains were falling to the waters below.

The scream silenced her fellows, silenced their own internal sorrow for it had pierced them to bone, even as she turned and stormed away into town none dared to move or cry themselves. Her father was loved, respected, feared; and died in a way not befit of such titles. Skal kept her head high but a roar in her throat. Eyes stinging as she felt her younger brother's tightened grip on her arm slip away and remain with the men.

    The town was silent, everyone left was at his funeral. They were there to be present as her father was sent to sail with the spirits of the sea. Skal's wispy wind hair thrashed in the wintry wind as she wandered in fury. Patterns of waves and air upon her arms swirling the sea's anger as she walked through the desolate town. She eyed the buildings; strong ships made to homes that were blasted when destruction sped through. The streets lined still with the bodies of brave men and women, covered in tattered clothes of red and blue, decorated with embroidered patterns of the sea. Slowly they morphed to plain white ones, tattered with holes which could not hide what was within. Ugly white cloth which lacked such patterns the further Skal got through her town's ruins. She gritted her teeth, angered by her fellows state.

    That mess of a power grab which took this all from her people, took away what was theirs; for an act of might to show off their status to others. That's what she'd heard them say when she pinned a soldier in the corner as his own fellows fled. It was a comment that had sent Skal's fury blazing and even now, she could smell that man's flesh in her nostrils. Skal seethed now with anger, the roar in her throat thirsty for release, yet she held it down.

Dragons bellowed in agony from the beach, she barely glanced as she felt the flames behind her. Dragons mourned in their own way, the ones burning flames were sending longing pleas to their riders who fell. They'd either stay or leave soon after; others would sail the sea with their riders once their mourning consumed them. Her father's warm jacket rested on her shoulders, the once piercing colour of red now a faded fiery orange. Wearing it made her feel closer to him, like he had her in a headlock and was whispering a joke in her ear. She'd longed for a joke right now, something to kill the storm which brewed about her town. Kill the forlorn fears of her fellows. Kill the ache in her mothers and brothers hearts.

But presently, there was no cure. Purely rage.

She'd hardly noticed the distance she'd walked and was now standing at the Deepened Shore. She looked down, walking slower and hearing the sand crunch and snap below her boots. Her arms folded into her pant pockets; she sneered at the sand. She avoided crabs but was sure to step on every rotting bone she saw. Deepend Shore had one purpose; when a prisoner had seen their use, or was dragged back for wronging them. This was where they belonged. Skal had been here many a time, always with her father, never alone. It was overlooking here on the cliffs, that she and her little brother received their armbands as all blood of the Reignherus do. Iron bands decorated with the Echo's waves and words, representations that the two had ascended fifteen.

That was last year for her brother. For her it was three years ago.

Building in Dead Sands
by Morgan McLean-Alexander

A sharp swing of her boot sent a skull flying to the dangerous blackened sea. Her arm patterns swirled more, the waves grew more aggressive as Skal paced then threw her head back. Locking gaze with the turbulent sky, her father's jacket hugging her as she stared up. Listening to the roar of the wind around her, and before she knew it; she was laughing. A manic, sane laugh. One that she'd never voiced before.

Skal fell back, crashing into the bone sand. Covering her eyes with her hands and laughing. Tears refused to come, soon another roaring scream escaped with the laughter. It was the same roar that had been boiling in her throat. She shot straight up as she roared, all the while feeling her father's fiery jacket around her. She sat there after it passed, slumped and glaring still at the sky.

"Echo bring me power, what a fucking mess this be," Skal snarled to herself.

She looked down at the sand, poking through the sand and finding small chunks of bone. The wind roared around her, as she soon uncovered a skull. She picked it up and smirked, it was just the top of some prisoner's head. She flipped it over in her hand, scooping the air with first a glare and then a grin. Her eyes fell as she looked to the sea, had a funny thought that flowed, and crawled over on her knees to the sea's shore. She stopped inches from the water, threw her father's coat from her shoulders to a pike in the ground behind her, and plunged the skull top in the sand.

Skal was digging in the sand, like she was with her friends at the beach as a nipper once more. Digging a trench and building a

Building in Dead Sands
by Morgan McLean-Alexander

mound in the middle. Longer pieces of bone proved to be good support for the island she built in the trench. She hummed a warriors tune, the sky still swirling but now without its roar. The waves thrashed once or twice more, yet soon settled. Skal sat back, with sand and bone bits up her arms and skull top in hand, she eyed her creation.

"What in the Depths of Crate are you doing?" Eivor said, Skal glanced in the direction of her brother's voice.

She looked back and laughed, "Digging!"

Her exclamation came with a hint of mania. A hint that she knew to hide, to present a persona she knew people would accept. She tilted her head, looking at the little island she made, waves growing closer to the trench as she did. The black waters melded with the black sand to create a trench for the little island. Upon the island of sand and bone, was a little town of mounds. She imagined each house a triangle with a sturdy roof, a market, a smith, the main hall like the one she'd known growing up.

"Yeah I see that, why are you digging?" Eivor asked as he walked up behind her.

Skal looked up, seeing her brother standing there. His arms were folded, a fresh bandage over the left half of his face, marking where some glass and flame took away some of his youth, leaving the tired dying part of him now easier to see. He looked nothing like her, with darkened skin and white hair tipped by violet streaks. His remaining eye was silver, flickering like a flame as he pointed at the town of sand and bone. Skal held up the skull top.

"Found a shovel."

Building in Dead Sands
by Morgan McLean-Alexander

"Where?"

"In the sand, mixed with the bones."

"Where?"

"Echo's sake, look."

"Oh found one."

"Good come join me!"

It was like they were kids once more. Eivor, without hesitation, was now digging in the sand with Skal. Her father's jacket's left arm flickered behind them, waving as though an arm were there. The duo expanded the town along the edge of the water, linking it to the sea which was calming as they worked. Skal found the odd skeletal remains, using bones to support structures of the island itself, and watching her brother use them instead to build better buildings. Soon they had more than a town on a single island. They had five islands, each made from the sand and surrounded by a trench formed from the siblings digging, and the sea's contribution of itself. Skal created all the landmasses and rough shapes, Eivor came along behind her and smoothed things out and added more structure and detail to each town and home. Skal knelt, admiring the work while looking at her makeshift shovel. Eivor walked over with their father's jacket, eyeing his sister as he handed it to her. She looked at the jacket fondly, eyes watering a little now.

He flopped it on her shoulders as she gazed back at the town of sand and bone. The jacket felt warmer. Skal stayed knelt in the sand as the jacket laid upon her shoulders, Eivor stood beside her. Arms folded, both gazing out to sea. Surrounded by the dead, not their dead.

Their dead rested with the Echo, the one who is both the strength and power of Skal's people. The wind gently brushed her still swirling hair, she heard drums behind her and shouting. Not angry shouting, just her people shouting an old song. They don't really sing, singing was for mainlanders. Her people would shout and chant in mourning; loud enough for the Echo, and dead to hear. A hand flopped on her head as a realization of the present and future penetrated her own mourning;

"Come on; mum needs us, so do the fellows," Eivor said.

Skal heard the crunching as he walked off, but her gaze was on the sea. Out to where their ships and Dragons longed to be. Out where fights were won or lost, mainlanders struggled while they flourished. It dawned on her that the future of the island and her people was hers. Hers to sculpt and guide in this world of loss and rumbling war. Skal grabbed the edge of the jacket, thinking of her father as she eyed the town of sand and bone. She felt his embrace around her; his boisterous laugh, and sharp wit in her ear. She felt his calloused hands on her shoulders, showing her the ships, how to hunt, hold an axe, stand and fight like a warrior, and skin a kill. She looked at her sand and bone towns. The islands. She slowly stood, slipping her arms in her father's jacket and laughing a strong, hardy laugh.

"Skal?" Eivor asked, she turned.

"Aye?"

"Quit, laughing... you sound like father."

Skal looked at him, at his sad silver eye and arms folded around himself in embrace. She smiled slowly, creating a sneer on her face as she turned to him, tilting her head.

"I got a plan Eivor," Skal said. Eivor stared as Skal walked away from the sand and bone; the feel of a cool, familiar hand holding Skal's shoulder as he said, "a plan for not us, but fer here."

"Oh?" Eivor questioned.

"Aye," Skal said as he walked by his brother, head held high and a laugh in his throat, "come on, let's go tell them fellows what we learned."

Crimson
by Sylvia Belcher

"My goddamn tights ripped, you got any?" Carla looks up at me. Cherry lips, frilly skirt, velvet corset squeezing her breasts to the spilling point. I sigh, opening the chest at the base of my bed in our shared room. I pull out a bright red pair, tossing them her way.
"Thanks a mill." Her plastered on beauty mark stretches when she smiles, not trying to mask her Cockney accent around me. I stride over to the mirror of our beaten up vanity pushed against the wall, smudging away a stray bit of mascara. Show time. We bounce down the stairs, through the door in the wall leading backstage. Dusty. Always dusty.

"Let's get going ladies, get your asses in place!" Edgar shouts, clapping his hands with every word. I flinch at each smack, shying away. The piano starts up jauntily and I pause for a moment before straining into a perky grin. We prance onto the stage, creaking beneath our light feet. The men hoot and whoop, I look over them all, the dark hazy masses, cigarette smoke filling the joint, into the clouded stage lights. I focus on the counts of the music as we dance and twirl across the stage.

One, two, "Hey babyface." Three, four, "Nice tits dolly." five, six, "They've gotten younger, whew." seven, eight. One two, "I'm having *her* later."

Crimson
by Sylvia Belcher

After four hours, it's time for the real money. I'm musky and slick from the dancing, my makeup sloppy and melted. They won't care. Show piece. Stand in. Fantasy. The nausea of it has long since subsided, the fire in my chest burned down to an ember.

I lay daintily on the overly dressed bed, hand under my head, hip hiked up appealingly. The man opens the door, sour with booze, paunchy, with blackened teeth. I track him with my siren eyes. Giggle. He approaches me greedily and I let my mind slowly drift away. To *Mimsy and Pop.*

"Come on Pop, we're almost to Mushroom Town!" Mimsy says, bouncing along in her green plaid dress, her bunny ears flopping with every step. Pop hops along behind, a bluebird in a straw hat, tied with a periwinkle ribbon.

"I'm coming, I'm coming!" She chirps. Mimsy's basket is overflowing with ripe strawberries and blackberries, to be shared with their friends, the Mushroom Folk.

My head hits the headboard.

"When we get to Mushroom Town, I'm sure Bella will have made fresh bread!" Pop tweets.

"Maybe tonight we can read each other bedtime stories!" Mimsy squeaks excitedly.

My head smacks against the headboard, harder.

As Mimsy and Pop skip down the path they hear a sudden growl.

Crimson
by Sylvia Belcher

"Oh no..." Mimsy whispers as they turn around slowly to see Brutus the bear ambling towards them, baring his massive canines, a red handkerchief adorning his thick neck.

Again, my head slams against the wood, angling my neck painfully.

Brutus the bear roars, loping towards Mimsy and Pop full speed. They hop down the path, squealing.

"Pop, you have to fly away!" Mimsy cries.

"I can't! I don't know how!" Pop sobs.

"Please Pop, you have to try!"

One final crack of my head against wood, and the man rolls over with a grunt. My shift is over. He lays there gasping while I get up, pulling on my tights and curtsying prettily, before heading up the stairs to wash. Mimsy and Pop slowly fade away.

My skin feels thick with grime despite my cleaning, but I settle down at the vanity, opening the drawer I've claimed for my own. I look down at my only three possessions that are truly mine, that aren't makeup and costumes. My childhood teddy from my Mama. A dagger, which she disapproved of but Father gave me anyway, before the accident, wrapped in red velvet I tore from one of my skirts. And most importantly, my pen and inkwell. I pull out my ink and pen to write down everything I'd dreamed tonight about *Mimsy and Pop*. My pen scratches at the creamy paper, words curling out, round and soft. I imagine how thrilled the children of London will be this Sunday, when they swing their legs with eager impatience at the

Crimson
by Sylvia Belcher

breakfast table waiting for their fathers to finish the newspaper. When the pages are finally placed down, they will be snatched up happily, and the next chapter will be devoured.

"Ellie, blow out the damn candle," Carla drawls as she slinks into the room. An unwashed and masculine scent rolling off of her as she collapses into her bed, frilly skirt still bunched up around her hips. I take one last glance at my page of words before extinguishing the candle, watching it gutter and go out, my stomach a pit to match the inky black that overtakes the dank space.

I'm up with the weak sunlight and back at the vanity, my pen already flying across a new page.

"Please Pop, you have to try!" Pop begins to flap her little wings as she runs, her periwinkle bow waving frantically.

"I can't! I can't!"

"Yes you can, I believe in you!" Shouts Mimsy, as Brutus growls menacingly behind them. "You have to fly and call for help!"

I glance at the clock, realize the time, and dress. Carla's rasping breaths fill the air as she sleeps, rattling and catching. A choking sound fills the room and she bolts upright.

"The fuck are you going at this hour?"

"Just to see a friend."

"Aww, do you have a little sweetheart?" I redden at the thought of such a thing. Much too intimate.

Crimson
by Sylvia Belcher

"I'll be back later." I turn away, grab my handbag, and rush down the stairs

"Eleanor, my girl!" I round the corner of Staton Street, ten blocks from the joint, to find Maurice waiting at our spot, under the apple tree. I break into a smile at the soft gray-haired man.

"I brought you the next installment," I say.

"Amazing, amazing! I had little James down the road here just yesterday, practically begging to find out what happens to Mimsy and Pop." My face flushes as I pull the pages from my bag, the ink long dried. I've had the newspaper installments finished months in advance so I could focus on my main project. I've been publishing these stories for a year now, under the guise of a male. Maurice is the quiet middleman. He found me one night a couple years ago. His wife had recently died and he was hitting the bottle as religiously as she had once attended church. One night, his face streaked with heavy tears and his body reeking of booze, it happened to be my room he was led to when he visited the establishment. Once. Only once did he ever indulge in such a thing. A week later he returned, found me, and begged for my forgiveness. He divulged that he worked at the newspaper and I proposed a way for him to apologize, a way that would no doubt ease the wrath of his late wife, I made sure to add. Ever since then my stories have appeared in the paper weekly–under the pseudonym of Edward Blight. I eventually piqued publishers' interest in a novel, and I've been writing feverishly in the months since, every waking moment.

Crimson
by Sylvia Belcher

"Can we talk about the novel? The publisher is getting impatient, Elle. You know I've stalled as long as I can. If it's not in by tomorrow morning, they're going to pull out of the deal. They wanted a draft a month ago. This flurry over your stories won't last forever."

"I'm almost done, Maurice, I promise. I'll bring it by tonight after my shift, at 12, so you can have it by morning."

He lets out a low sigh. "Fine."

He reaches his hand into his pocket and pulls out a handful of coins. He drops them into my waiting palm. They're warm. Mine. Honest. I hurry back to make the most of my afternoon hours.

Pop's wings keep flapping with absolute desperation. She's crying now, little tears falling down her beak.

"I can't do it!" Brutus is close behind, his red handkerchief all Mimsy can see as she runs up behind Pop.

"I've got you!" Mimsy yells as she throws her basket of berries towards Brutus, places her hands around Pop's tummy, and pushes her up into the sky.

Dusk falls over the city, thick and heavy. I cake on heavy foundation, layer after layer to hide my soft freckles and the ever-darkening circles around my eyes. Deep rouge. Crimson lips. A clown. That old nausea bubbles up in my chest. I push it down. I'm all angles these days. Not sensual in my curves the way Carla is. Like a child who got into her mother's makeup. Playing pretend. Always playing pretend.

Crimson
by Sylvia Belcher

"Eleanor." I look up from the mirror to see Edgar, long black coat and matching hat. I notice a red rose at his lapel. I nod, bashful in his presence. "My angel. I can't help but notice you've been a little off on your choreography lately." His voice is velvety, the kind of velvet that wraps around sharpness.

"I'm sorry," I stammer. "I guess I've just been tired."

"You can't afford to be tired, lovely. There are girls on the street practically begging to be in your position." The ember in my chest flares. I put it out.

"Of course, I'm so sorry." I say, lowering my head.

"And by the way," He drawls. "Inflation is up. Next month, rent doubles. So start stretching."

We burst on stage. My skirts fan out around me as I whip across the stage, frenzied. One two three, one two three, one two three. My heartbeat thumps in my ears, blood pulsing deeply, drowning out the profane voices. Harsh stage lights, dust, sweat, velvet and red.

I once again assemble myself on the elaborate bed, awaiting yet another patron. I watch the clock as I wait for the door to open. 8 pm. Four hours to 12, and my last chapter is sitting unfinished in my desk drawer. The door opens to a tall man, stringy black hair falling around his face.

9:00 pm. The next man comes in, portly, ruddy and blond.

Crimson
by Sylvia Belcher

As Mimsy gives Pop a boost she begins to gain a little bit of air.

"You're doing it! Keep going while he's distracted by the berries!" Mimsy cries. Brutus the Bear scarfs down the berries, so so hungry.

Pop keeps flapping, going up, up, up. "I'm doing it!"

"Yes Pop! You've got this!" Pop flaps harder and harder, but her small wings grow tired. She begins losing air, and tumbles to the ground, rolling. "I can't!" She wails.

10:00pm Red hair and spectacles.

Brutus devours every last berry in his basket, then slowly looks up at Pop fallen on the ground ahead, and Mimsy helping her up.

"I'm hungry." Brutus growls. "Hungry for little soft ones."

Pop shrieks and gets to her tiny feet, running, running desperately, her wings moving up and down so so quickly. She begins to take off, begins to fly.

Mimsy keeps hopping, "Keep going, don't stop until Mushroom Town!" Pop is flying now, properly. Up above the path, up above the trees, until she disappears from sight. Mimsy realizes she's alone now. Alone with a hungry bear barreling towards her.

11:00pm: An old man. A hungry old man.

Crimson
by Sylvia Belcher

Mimsy takes off down the path, her little heart beating far faster than any bunny's should ever have to. She hops and hops and hops, the hot breath and huge body of Brutus behind her fuelling her forwards.

"Please," She whimpers as she runs. "Please." She hops and hops and hops, her small haunches burning, her pink nose hot and runny. She feels Brutus's fur brush against her back, and she braces herself for that big, hungry mouth.

The rickety man leaves as the clock hits 11:30. I have to go, there's no time. I rush to collect myself and push open the door, rushing up the little set of stairs.

"Eleanor."

I turn around slowly. "You're not going to leave this nice man waiting are you?"

Edgar stands with yet another man who is merely disjointed features to me.

"Edgar…I can't."

His face stills before smiling coldly.

"Oh, I think you can."

"No, Edgar. Please."

"Eleanor." His voice is calm, icy.

I stand on the stairs, breathing deeply, my pages and future waiting above, the open door to the bedroom below.

"Can you just get me a different one?" The man with Edgar asks.

Crimson
by Sylvia Belcher

"Eleanor." He's less quiet this time.

I begin to burn. The ember flaring. I stifle it, as my eyes become hot and wet and I step gingerly back down the stairs, into that tomb of a room.

I hold back tears, smacking into that headboard again and again. Lifeless.

Bang. Bang. Bang. He crashes into me. Through me. Devouring me.

Done. I push the man's gasping body off of my own, whipping open the door and sprinting for my room. I get to the vanity, grabbing my pen desperately. But words don't come. The reservoir of ink inside me is dry. No, no, no. It's 12. The tears begin again, burning as they trail down my cheeks, cutting ebony ravines of eyeliner into my facade of foundation. Sobs begin to wrack my frail body, painful. I look up at myself in the mirror. A dress up doll. The words won't come. *Mimsy and Pop* is a story of innocence. Hope. The place where those things once laid is barren. I am a cemetery, the kind filled with too small graves and stuffed toys. That ember in my chest begins to flare and for once I don't put it out. I feel the flames ravage my body, but not the way I am usually ravaged each night. I am taken completely. I fumble open my drawer in the vanity, finding the crimson handkerchief, and the sharpness it hides beneath. I slip it under my skirt, under my garter, and head for the door. My head fills

Crimson
by Sylvia Belcher

with smoke. I step down the stairs slowly, purposefully. Heading backstage.

I peer out to the stage. Girls on the late shift, a rolling mass of undulating bodies, twisting and kicking. A sick display of oily ballet. The shouts in the crowd become louder, hooting, hollering. The air is thick with boozy breath. Someone vomits. The girls perform their last section, a can-can, before waltzing off-stage. I push past them, and walk purposefully to the centre of the empty stage. The crowd begins hollering again, and I look to the pianoman's surprised face. I smile and nod confidently, as if I was born to be here. I search through the roiling crowd and lock eyes with Edgar, always somewhere as a spectator. Orchestrating. Watching.

"This one is for a special friend. An apology." I project.
The pianoman starts up a sultry melody, and I dance. Not my usual choreography. I let myself burn. I'm a raging pillar of consuming flame as I move, wild, uneasy, dangerous. The crowd grows quieter as my movements become sharper, more feral, unrestrained. I dance for what feels like hours. I burn. Burn. Burn. When I am at my peak, at the climax, when I am an inferno, I jump from the stage to the crowd below. They stumble back in surprise, and instead of rushing towards me as they normally might have, they part for me, a red sea of bodies, as I walk straight for Edgar. He's smiling. Not cold anymore. Surprised...hungry.

"My, my," he murmurs. "Our quiet and shy little girl is coming out of her shell." I walk close to him, brushing just past, and grinning over my shoulder, beckoning. I walk through the crowd back towards the hallway, Edgar following. The crowd begins to whoop again as some new spectacle takes the stage.

I lead him not to my room of work, but to my own bedroom. His eyes are glazed as he follows. I lay him down on my small bed. He looks disproportionate, a monstrosity in my simple space. I burn.

"I'm sorry for earlier," I say coyly. "I hope I can make it up to you."

"I'm sure you can," he breathes.

I strut towards him, running a finger down his chest to his buttons. I undo them, taking my time, one by one. His breaths become deep. I kiss his mouth as I reach down to my garter and take hold of the dagger's hilt.

"Thank you for saving me from the big scary world Edgar." I pull away to see that self-righteous look one last time before driving my dagger directly into his pulsing heart.

I sit at my desk, my ink jar full. The words come at last.

Just as Brutus's mouth opens to engulf Mimsy, she spins around, kicking up one powerful foot into the snout of the bear. He roars in pain, stumbling back. Mimsy hops ever-forward, her foot aching, and her body exhausted.

"Mimsy!!" Mimsy looks up to the sky to see Pop, soaring down. Pop tosses a net down onto the charging bear. Mimsy lets out a sob of relief as her friends emerge from the woods to help capture Brutus and take her home.

Crimson
by Sylvia Belcher

"Wait." She says to her friends before they can. Mimsy walks up slowly to the bear. He is now helpless, vulnerable. She gets close to him, so close to him, before ripping off the red bandana around his neck. Her friends cheer, Pop the loudest.

And they all lived happily ever after.

The final words of my novel glint on the page, dripping the deepest crimson.

CONTRIBUTOR BIOGRAPHIES

Bailey J. Wilson is a Queer, disabled writer attempting to navigate life through her writing. She is the incoming Vice President of Administrative Affairs for Write Club and an English major working towards her BA at Mount Royal University in Calgary, Alberta. Bailey enjoys writing both fiction and poetry and tries to infuse her works with a touch of humour. She is a fan of the fantasy and science fiction genres, currently working on a story based on Celtic mythology. In her spare time, Bailey enjoys video games, reading, drawing, board games, and video editing.

Emma Marion is a 21-year-old Canadian writer, and a second year student at Mount Royal University, pursuing a degree in the Education program. She is Write Club's incoming Vice President of Newsletters. Emma has always had a passion for writing and sharing stories, and loves exploring new ways to put her ideas down on a page. The main genre of these works is fiction and romance, though she has two non-fiction projects in workshop, while also hoping to explore the Western subgenre more. Emma has a lengthy list of hobbies and activities she loves to take part in, such as volunteering with the Girl Guides of Canada, playing video games, camping, vinyl collecting, and so much more. Her biggest inspirations come from her family members, especially her mother and sisters, with honorable mentions going to her dog Nikki, and cats Mabel and Phyllis.

CONTRIBUTOR BIOGRAPHIES

Chandler Christie was born in 1995 and grew up in Nanton, Alberta where his interest in creative writing flourished from an interest in general science fiction. After graduating, he was inspired to enroll at MRU to develop his authorial skills, where he participated in the honours seminar. He currently lives in Calgary, where he is intent on becoming a fully-fledged author, with several other works in progress ongoing and continues to develop his craft. Chandler is grateful for his family, who have been supportive of his creative endeavours, and of his studies that have enabled him to express why creative freedom is important in today's modern media landscape.

Sylvia Belcher is in her second year at Mount Royal and the incoming Vice President of Fundraising for Write Club, studying psychology. She has always been a passionate writer, telling stories for as long as she could talk. She loves to write poetry and fiction, spanning any genre she finds interesting at the time. When Sylvia isn't writing she can be found in nature, as you can no doubt guess from much of her writing.

Spencer Heindle is a fourth-year English Major with a Minor in Creative Writing. When she first applied to MRU, she genuinely had no idea what she was passionate about and taking English was just a shot in the dark. She was always told that she had such a creative outlook on life and that creativity won't make for a stable job- unless she got lucky. This advice lit a flame of desire within her to prove those people wrong. However, most of her early classes focused on literature through an analytical lens. By her second year of university, she was convinced her purpose in life was to have no purpose. Then she discovered poetry. A genre of creative writing which she once believed was too advanced felt like home, as if all this time she had been sitting on the puzzle piece she had been searching for.

Dovonna Meloche is an Indigenous (Ojibwe) writer from Naotkamegwanning First Nation (Treaty #3) pursuing a Bachelor of Arts in English at Mount Royal University. She enjoys writing fiction and poetry and aspires to one day publish a novel. Genres that Dovonna enjoys writing include fantasy, romance, and mystery/thriller. Projects she is currently working on are a murder mystery novel and a fantasy trilogy. For Dovonna, writing is a way of processing, a way of getting out overwhelming emotions, and healing. Writing is Mino-mashkikiiwan, good medicine.

Myra Munday has been writing freeform poetry since around 2021. Poetry is how she began to understand her emotions and her love for writing has slowly grown from there. Her poems are written from her own experiences, thoughts and feelings which she shares in hope someone else might benefit from them.

Levi Neighbour is the incoming Master of Ceremonies for Write Club and is currently a student at Mount Royal University, hoping to graduate with honours in 2026. He dreams of becoming a music teacher to inspire a future generation with his passion for music and the arts. When he is not busy spending way too much money on comic books or tattoos, Levi enjoys playing music in his band, being a nerd, or enjoying his time outdoors from the safety of the shade.

Elle Nyitrai is a writer born and raised in Calgary, Alberta. She is currently a second-year student pursuing her BA with a major in English at Mount

Royal University. Her work has been published in FreeFall magazine, and she has been awarded the Micheline Maylor Prize for Poetic Excellence.

Teresa Anderson is a licensed practical nurse most days, a student some days, and a writer by night. Currently in third year, she pursues a BA in English with an interest in creative writing. One day, she would like to become an editor. One day, she would like to write a novel. For now, fulfillment is found by writing every day, even if she can only manage a sentence. She was born and raised in Calgary, and lives with her husband, son, and dog.

Chau Luong is a university student with a mixed Filipino and Vietnamese heritage, being born in the Philippines. She is currently pursuing studies in both English and Accounting, blending her analytical skills with her creative passions. An avid writer and artist, Chau finds solace and inspiration in creativity, using it as a balance to the structure of her academic pursuits. With a love for nature and exploration, she enjoys hiking and discovering the world's natural wonders. Chau's dedication to her studies is reflected in her consistent achievement of being on the President's Honor Roll, and she is thrilled about her upcoming study abroad experience in Spain.

Driven by a deep appreciation for life, she seeks to connect with people and experiences that challenge and expand her perspectives. Chau aspires to inspire others to embrace life's beauty, even in its difficulties, and to live fully and authentically.

Levi Lewko is an avid writer from the Calgary Area with a fondness for writing fiction. His works often employ humour and a lighthearted, comedic tone that is often described as campy to provide the reader with an enjoyable experience. His works can often range in genre; anywhere from horror, to western, to fantasy.

Christina Jarmics is the Secretary and upcoming President of the Write Club and a first year Business student at Mount Royal University. Her childhood was filled with literature and writing which drove the passion she has now for branching out and creating poetry herself. Christina was born and raised in Calgary and most of her written work is related to her own experiences, friends and the places around her.

Franz Valencia is an anthropology student at Mount Royal University and the incoming Vice President of Finances for Write Club and has been a fan of books for most of his life. Fiction is his favorite type of books to read and write, with a special interest in fantasy, science fiction, horror and the weird. In his spare time, as much as he'd like to read or write, he usually just lazes around and does nothing of note.

Mel Perez: "Hiya, I'm Mel, just your friendly neighbourhood human trying to figure things out, in my last year at university with writing keeping me sane >:) I still enjoy indie games (life is strange double exposure right now), daydreaming to music, my people/loved ones, and spoken word poetry that make me or others cry/laugh, hopefully, both:) Be kind to yourself <3" -Mel ... XD

Mark (Marcus) Vertodazo is a Filipino Canadian born in Calgary and raised within the South East neighborhoods of Forest Lawn. He is a full-time student at Mount Royal University, majoring in Sociology while pursuing a minor in Creative Writing. Creatively, he identifies first as a Spoken Word Poet. He is also currently the VP of Outreach and Relations for MRU's Write Club. In his free time, Marcus spends his days getting lost in random neighborhoods on his skateboard, loitering in libraries and bookstores, and binge listening to an artist's entire discography. His overall dream is to become an officially recognized poet laureate.

B. Kenneth Brown is a Queer Métis writer, scholar, and open-source web developer serving as the Founder and outgoing President of the Write Club. Currently completing his English Honours at Mount Royal University, his academic work explores Indigenous resilience, identity, and narrative sovereignty. His recently published research in the Mount Royal Undergraduate Humanities Review examines Indigenous representation in graphic novels.

As a poet, Brown's debut chapbook *Holy Waterfall: 16 New & Selected Poems for Mohkínstsis akápiyoyis & the Red River* (2023) weaves together themes of Indigenous identity, spirituality, and personal transformation. Through confessional poetry and outsider art, his work creates spaces for healing and celebration while exploring the intersections of Queer and Indigenous perspectives.

Combining his passion for literature with community development, Brown dedicates himself to empowering marginalized voices and creating lasting impact through storytelling. Whether developing innovative content strategies or fostering community engagement, he approaches each project with analytical insight and collaborative spirit.

J.R. Adamson is a Canadian writer and musician currently residing in Calgary, Alberta. His debut poetry collection, *I'm Just Waiting for*

Something to Happen, which challenges the coming-of-age narrative, was co-created with his esteemed colleague, collaborator, and friend, Felix da Costa Gomez. Adamson's writing confronts and tackles a variety of topics such as human connection, isolation, alienation, and the brutal realities of everyday life.

Felix Da Costa Gomez is a fourth year English Honours student at Mount Royal University, and he specializes in works of fiction and poetry. In the Fall of 2023, he co-authored a poetry book titled *I'm Just Waiting for Something to Happen* with his friend and peer Jake Beka, and he is currently working on his western trilogy Extermination Project. With hopes to someday be acknowledged as a prolific author, Felix's main passion has to do with creative writing.

Ademola Adesola is an assistant professor in the Department of English, Languages, and Cultures, at Mount Royal University, Canada. Ademola teaches and researches postcolonial literatures, African and Black Diaspora literatures, children and warfare, and human rights issues.

Morgan McLean Alexander is the incoming Vice President of Innovation and Ideation for Write Club and a Calgary native with a passion for mythology and world building within stories. Morgan has a special interest in the myths of Asia, as well as the Norse legends of Yggdrasil. Having dealt with anxiety and depression her whole life she tends to write characters with complicated pasts who find comfort in found families. She is presently working on the first novel in a series she hopes to complete later this year, while also studying English and Creative Writing.

CONTRIBUTOR BIOGRAPHIES

Rachel Fitzgibbon is the incoming Social Media Coordinator for Write Club and a Calgary born writer with a focus on poetry and prose. Her work is inspired by her life experiences, mythology, connection, and the human condition. She is in her second year at Mount Royal University. Outside of school she works in the film industry and spends her free time watching movies, reading books, and cuddling with her dog, Rusty.

Corbyn Andre is an English Honours Student at MRU. Corbyn focuses on critical theory, editing, and creative writing. His academic interests span multicultural literature and nineteenth-century studies, deconstructing tropes within genre, and aspires toward a career in English education at secondary level while pursuing personal writing projects.

ABOUT WRITE CLUB

Mount Royal University's write club is a Creative Writing Club dedicated to nurturing the literary talents of our community in a safe and inclusive environment. Whether you're an experienced writer or a beginner embarking on your creative journey, our club offers a supportive space for you to hone your craft, share your work, and connect with like-minded individuals.

You can find more information at our website at https://writeclub.ca/ or our Instagram @writeclubmru.

Manufactured by Amazon.ca
Bolton, ON